"Meet me tonight at seven o'clock to discuss the job."

The one night Nina had restrictions. "The kids and I are serving dinner at my grandmother's senior center, and I can't cancel."

The pause on the other end of the line was brief. "Give me an address and a time, and I'll meet you there. You can ask your questions or watch me wash dishes."

After hanging up, Nina amended her opinion of David Hanson. He was wily and persistent and surprisingly skilled at getting his way. She wasn't sure what else she was going to discover about David tonight or how it would affect her decision to take the job. But suddenly that was not her greatest worry.

She was far more concerned with all the things she was discovering about herself when David was around.

Dear Reader,

Well, if there were ever a month that screamed for a good love story—make that six!—February would be it. So here are our Valentine's Day gifts to you from Silhouette Special Edition. Let's start with *The Road to Reunion* by Gina Wilkins, next up in her FAMILY FOUND series. When the beautiful daughter of the couple who raised him tries to get a taciturn cowboy to come home for a family reunion, Kyle Reeves is determined to turn her down. But try getting Molly Walker to take no for an answer! In Marie Ferrarella's *Husbands and Other Strangers,* a woman in a boating accident finds her head injury left her with no permanent effects—except for the fact that she can't seem to recall her husband. In the next installment of our FAMILY BUSINESS continuity, *The Boss and Miss Baxter* by Wendy Warren, an unemployed single mother is offered a job—not to mention a place to live for her and her children—with the grumpy, if gorgeous, man who fired her!

"Who's Your Daddy?" is a question that takes on new meaning when a young woman learns that a rock star is her biological father, that her mother is really in love with his brother—and that she herself can't resist her new father's protégé. Read all about it in *It Runs in the Family* by Patricia Kay, the second in her CALLIE'S CORNER CAFÉ miniseries. *Vermont Valentine,* the conclusion to Kristin Hardy's HOLIDAY HEARTS miniseries, tells the story of the last single Trask brother, Jacob—he's been alone for thirty-six years. But that's about to change, courtesy of the beautiful scientist now doing research on his property. And in Teresa Hill's *A Little Bit Engaged,* a woman who's been a bride-to-be for five years yet never saw fit to actually set a wedding date finds true love where she least expects it—with a pastor.

So keep warm, stay romantic, and we'll see you next month....

Gail Chasan
Senior Editor

Please address questions and book requests to:
Silhouette Reader Service
U.S.: 3010 Walden Ave., P.O. Box 1325, Buffalo, NY 14269
Canadian: P.O. Box 609, Fort Erie, Ont. L2A 5X3

THE BOSS AND MISS BAXTER

WENDY WARREN

Silhouette®

SPECIAL EDITION

Published by Silhouette Books

America's Publisher of Contemporary Romance

Special thanks and acknowledgement
are given to Wendy Warren for her
contribution to the Family Business series.

 SILHOUETTE BOOKS

ISBN 0-373-24737-0

THE BOSS AND MISS BAXTER

WENDY WARREN

lives with her husband, Tim, a dog, a cat and their recent—and most exciting!—addition, baby daughter Elisabeth, near the Pacific Northwest's beautiful Willamette River. Their house was previously owned by a woman named Cinderella, who bequeathed them a gardenful of flowers they try desperately (and occasionally successfully) not to kill, and a pink General Electric oven, circa 1958, that makes the kitchen look like an *I Love Lucy* rerun.

A two-time recipient of the Romance Writers of America's RITA® Award for Best Traditional Romance, Wendy loves to read and write the kind of books that remind her of the old movies she grew up watching with her mom—stories about decent people looking for the love that can make an ordinary life heroic. Wendy was an *Affaire de Coeur* finalist for Best Up and Coming Romance Author of 1997. When not writing, she likes to take long walks with her dog, settle in for cozy chats with good friends and sneak tofu into her husband's dinner. She always enjoys hearing from readers, and may be reached at P.O. Box 1208, Ashland, OR 97520.

For Patricia Giacolini, as beautiful a friend as she is a poet. With all my heart, thank you for being Libbi's auntie and playmate so I could finish this book! And thank you for gifting your friends with the grace and wisdom of your elegant words.

Chapter One

"Tell *no one* that I did this."

"It's between us. I swear." Nina Baxter smiled at her friend and former co-worker. The smile felt forced and phony, but at least the words were sincere.

Burying her bunched fists more deeply into the pockets of her jacket, Nina stood by as Carolyn Ahearn fitted her master key into a polished brass doorknob and unlocked the heavy oak doors protecting Hanson Media from the rest of the world.

Nina felt her stomach clench as the door eased open. She'd crossed this threshold countless times over the past thirteen years—five days a week, Monday through Friday—but couldn't remember ever being here on a Sunday.

Nor could she recall ever being this nauseous when she'd come to work, and that included the months she'd slogged through morning sickness.

"I'm going to make a run to Noah's for a bagel and latte," Carolyn said, pocketing the key. "It'll probably take twenty minutes. Is that enough time?"

Nina nodded. "I'll meet you back here." She reached out to take her friend's hand. "I can't thank you enough, Carolyn. I'm sorry you had to interrupt your weekend for me. I just couldn't face—"

"I know." Giving Nina's cold fingers a reassuring squeeze, Carolyn shrugged. "It could have been you opening the door for me, kiddo. It was just the luck of the draw. Layoffs bite."

Nina's laugh sounded watery. "Big-time." She'd been *laid off* on Friday, told she could come back to collect her things on Monday if she needed to, but she wanted to wave goodbye with a modicum of grace—not stumble to the elevators with her arms full of items from her desk, and her eyes bloodshot and teary.

Even now, as tears gathered at the back of her throat, she clung to her stiff upper lip like a drowning man to a life preserver. "Go eat a bagel," she told Carolyn. "Extra cream cheese."

"Oh, sure," Carolyn mumbled as she turned back toward the elevators that had carried them to the offices of Hanson Media Group. "Easy for you to say. You can't eat when you're stressed. I devour my weight in carbs." She walked down the lushly carpeted hallway without looking back, and Nina quietly shut the door, listening for the click that locked her in.

With what she hoped was poetic dignity, she made her way past the imposing reception desk against the wall that sported a huge gold *H* in a circle, and continued round to the circular bank of desks where the secretaries worked.

Hanson Media Group had been her home away from home since she'd first walked through the doors at nineteen—newly married, delighted to start her first "real" job and pregnant with her first child. The clerical position she'd applied for had required office skills she hadn't possessed at the time and formal business attire she hadn't owned. She should have been daunted by the opulent surroundings and by co-workers who had made her look like a junior high intern. But Nina had needed the job too much to let a little intimidation thwart her. And she had been naive then. Wonderfully, happily naive.

Arriving at the desk that had become hers the day she'd been promoted to secretary, Nina trailed her fingers mournfully over the nubby back of her ergonomically correct chair. Monday through Friday, no matter what insanity had pervaded her personal life, she'd had this chair to sit down on, this desk to work at. She'd had self-respect—a single mom making a living and securing the future for herself and her kids.

All gone. All the security, everything she'd worked for—gone in one lightning-swift chop of the corporate guillotine.

A rush of anxiety made Nina feel as if she were about to internally combust. Her nausea intensified. Trying to cool off, she discarded her coat, pulled a knitted purple hat off her head and got down to business.

Opening the large shoulder bag she'd brought with her, she began to stuff personal items inside. Two pictures of her kids...her favorite pens...the lavender notepad in the shape of a hippo... She moved rapidly, packing her purse at random until she came to the plastic gold trophy cup her daughter had given her last year after the annual Take Your Daughter to Work Day. World's Best Secretary.

Perusing the packed in-box and watching her mother's fingers fly across the computer keyboard, Isabella had looked at Nina with such respect that Nina had thought she could have been standing atop an Olympic podium—she'd felt that triumphant, that proud.

Suddenly her hands began to shake. She pushed the trophy into the depths of her bag and kept packing, but she couldn't stop shaking. Nor could she halt the anger that sparked like flash fire in her belly.

It wasn't *her* fault that Hanson Media was in trouble. It wasn't the fault of anyone who'd been laid off. The trouble had started at the top, but did the big dogs care about that? No. Even when they dug their own holes, it was the little guy who wound up with a mouthful of dirt.

And what had Nina done on Friday after being let go? She'd hugged her supervisor. That's right. She'd felt sorry for her obviously stressed supervisor, told her not to worry then brought her two aspirins and a glass of water.

Such a faithful employee; such a thoughtful person.

"Such a *doormat!*" Nina growled, feeling a surge of power that came from resentment, pure and simple. Who at Hanson would bring her an aspirin when she got a headache from searching the classifieds? Who would care whether she got a job before she had to move her kids' bedroom to the back seat of their Toyota?

"No one!" Nina answered her own question. And even though it was not nice, even though it was downright *wrong,* she picked up the first thing she spied—a plastic container filled with multicolored paper clips—and threw it as hard as she could against the solid oak door of David Hanson's office.

He was a big dog—emphasis on *dog*. He was a Hanson. Would he skip even one steak while his laid-off employees stocked up on Cup-a-Soup?

The paper-clip container made a satisfying *ping* against the door, but it wasn't nearly satisfying enough. So Nina picked up her Strunk and White's *The Elements of Style* and threw that against the door as well. Then she reached for her *Pocket Roget's Thesaurus*.

With each article she grabbed—and hurled—she said a naughty, naughty word she'd never used before.

And began to feel a little bit better.

"What the—"

David Hanson looked up from the paperwork covering his desk and stared at his closed office door. At first he'd thought someone was knocking—strange enough on a Sunday—but when he heard thwack after thwack against the solid wood, he realized he'd heard not a *knock* but a *smack*.

There was someone in the outer office, and that someone was throwing things at his door.

David didn't take long to think, and he didn't pause to consider calling reinforcements, like someone from building security. He rose, strode to the door and stood by, waiting for a lull in the assault. When it came, he jerked open the door....

And was almost decapitated by a stainless-steel travel mug.

"Holy—!" A timely duck saved him. Straightening, he locked eyes with a wild-haired blonde whose pitching arm was poised again. "Whoa!" David ordered, raising a hand to halt the action. When she froze, he turned his open hand into a warning index finger. "Excuse me. What the hell is going on out here?"

The blonde seemed incapable of speech. Or of

moving at all now that she'd been caught in the act of vandalizing his office.

David took a quick glance around. She was definitely alone, which he supposed was a good thing: one of her, one of him. Next, he noted that she had a strong arm (stood a good thirty feet from his door and still managed impressive velocity). And finally, he saw that she needed a tissue.

Tears filled the woman's eyes and streaked her face; her nose was red, and her cheeks were rapidly turning the same fiery shade. She looked so miserable, in fact, that he began to feel sorry for her until he reminded himself she was a vandal. He really ought to let security handle this. With all the other trouble he had right now, he didn't need a nutcase on his hands. He stepped one foot back toward his office. But then…

David leaned forward. And squinted. "Miss Baxter?"

With her arm still poised, the blonde blinked several times rapidly to clear her eyes. She attempted a smile that wobbled treacherously around the edges. "Yes?"

Jeez, it was her. He'd been thrown off by the exploding-firecracker effect of kinky blond curls and clothing that was more suited to a swap meet than the office. The Miss Baxter he was used to seeing during the week wore suits or skirts and blouses, like the other secretaries, and she wore her hair…well, hell, he couldn't really recall…in a bun?

David frowned. "What are you doing?" He was going to add *here,* but *what are you doing* seemed more apropos under the circumstances.

To her credit, she was obviously determined to make the best of the situation and shrugged with what appeared to be a miniature potted plant in her still-raised hand. "Cleaning."

He looked at the floor outside his door. A small paper-clip explosion had occurred; plus, there were two books and a silver mug lying on the carpet. "Cleaning?"

"My…desk…off. Sir."

After three of the most difficult and unpredictable months in his career, David should have been used to expecting the unexpected. But Nina Baxter had him knocked for a loop. Had there always been a psych case lurking behind the face of the mild-mannered secretary?

And then David realized…

Aw, hell.

Nina Baxter was one of the casualties of his late brother's screwups.

David squeezed the bridge of his nose as the headache he'd been battling for days took a sudden turn for the worse. Obviously he was not going to escape the mess his life had turned into. Not even on a Sunday.

While David Hanson hid behind his hand, Nina thought of the job reference she'd been counting on and figured she ought to start rehearsing, "Would you like fries with that?" as soon as possible.

Good God in heaven, what had she been thinking? Lowering her hand, she stared at the potted cactus her grandmother had given her. She was not a violent person. And yet she'd been about to smash the bit of flora into David Hanson's unsuspecting head. What if she'd already thrown the plant by the time he'd opened his door? The tiny needles could have lodged anywhere.

"I could have killed you!" The words burst out of her.

Obviously self-control was not her forte this morning. David Hanson's expression had already changed from anger to frowning distrust.

Note to self: Forget leaving Hanson Media Group with grace and dignity. She wasn't even going to look *sane*.

And if Mr. Hanson discovered how she'd gotten into the office, poor Carolyn might wind up in the unemployment line right behind her.

"I'm so terribly sorry," she said, rushing toward the scattered paper clips and other office weaponry. The closer she got to David Hanson, the more the sound of the ocean filled her ears. She had never felt comfortable in his presence, not in over a dozen years of working around him. In fact, she often avoided him when she could. He was so formal, always polite and correct and distant.

And tall. He was a good ten inches taller than her five foot three, and she had this thing about tall men. Fear of height.

"I'll clean up this mess and—" Realizing she still had the cactus in her hand, Nina looked for someplace to set it.

Surprising her, David reached for the pot. When their fingers brushed, she jumped at the contact and let go. He caught the plant in a deft save and stared down at her.

"Miss Baxter, may I suggest you sit down." He pointed to one of the desks several feet away from him. "Over there."

Yep, he thought she was crazy.

"I'm not usually like this," she said in her own defense. "Really. I'm usually calm. It's just that today I…" She searched for the correct word, for some way to explain her change from composed and trustworthy to certifiably wacko. "I'm very…"

Nina's mind scanned the options…*tired…worried…nervous?*

All accurate, but when her exhausted brain landed on exactly the right adjective, she knew it because her chest nearly burst with the effort to contain her grief, and her stomach pitched. Perhaps she shouldn't have said anything else at that point, but her body seemed to bring the words up of its own volition.

"It's just that I'm very…*UNEMPLOYED!*"

The tears she'd thus far managed to keep at bay

began spouting like geysers. Through them she spied David reaching out a hand. She pulled back before he could touch her.

Diving to the floor, she gathered the scattered paper clips, every last one, and the books and the mug. David watched her silently. The paper-clip container had obviously broken, and she wasn't sure where the pieces were, so she held out her fist.

"These…paper clips," she said, trying not to do that humiliating hiccup-sob thing, "are…not…mine."

When he made no move to take the clips, she pressed them into the soil around the cactus. Then she indicated the books. "These…*hic*…are mine."

David raised a brow. "Okay."

Nina turned and marched back to her desk. Grabbing the few remaining personal items, she stowed them in her bag, zipped it shut and snatched her coat and hat. She heard David call out, "Miss Baxter," but knew she had to get out before she broke down completely or Carolyn returned or both, so she picked up her pace and scurried to the outer doors—which was when she remembered that she was locked in and that Carolyn had the key.

It seemed like a good time to consider which window she could hurl herself from, but then David reached in front of her, slipped his own key into the lock and said, "Should I ask how you got in?"

Wordlessly she shook her head.

"Miss Baxter, I—"

Nina didn't wait. Ignoring the elevators, she hit the stairs running, fleeing like Cinderella from the ball.

For thirteen years, despite numerous challenges, she had maintained a spotless employment record and earned the respect of her co-workers. On Friday the clock had struck midnight. Now, two days later, she knew the party was over for good.

When Nina opened the door to her own apartment, the first thing she noticed was the aroma of chicken soup and something baking.

After telling Carolyn that she'd "run into" David Hanson, but that he didn't know who had let her into the office, she had walked around downtown Chicago for half an hour then bought a Sunday paper, a package of Rolaids and caught the El home. Before her stop, she'd wiped her eyes, blown her nose and applied a little lipstick to offset her red cheeks and bloodshot eyes. She hadn't eaten anything all day, and she still didn't want to, but she was determined to put up a good front for her family.

"I'm home!" she called into the quiet apartment.

As if her announcement had released a herd of gazelle, Nina's two children ran into the living room from opposite ends of the apartment. As always, they managed to sound as if, between them, they had ten pairs of feet rather than two.

Isabella arrived first, wrapping her arms around

her mother's waist and craning her head to look up. "I helped Bubby make matzo balls and *mandelbrodt!*" The exuberant ten-year-old's dark blue eyes sparkled with pride. "And guess what? Bubby says these matzo balls are lighter than air 'cause I have just the right touch!"

Nina smoothed a hand over Isabella's brown hair, gloriously wavy, but not frizzy like her own. "I can't wait to taste these matzo balls," she told her daughter. "Did you save me any?"

"We haven't eaten lunch yet." Isabella stepped back, making room for her brother, Isaac—Zach for short—to greet his mother. "I'm going to help Bubby some more." She loped back to the kitchen, preteen awkwardness and grace rolled into one lean body.

Nina looked at her son. At twelve years of age, Zach was old enough to contain his enthusiasm over seeing his mother a mere two hours after he'd last seen her. He stood back a bit, more interested in the *Chicago Sun-Times* than in Nina's return.

"Hi, Mom. Can I have the sports section?"

"Sure, honey." Stepping forward to run a hand over his short-cropped curls—because she wasn't too old to exhibit enthusiasm over seeing her son—Nina asked, "How were you today, Zachie? Any problems?"

Increasingly impatient of late when asked about his health, Zach ducked away from his mother's touch. "I'm *fine.*" He reached for the paper. "I want the movie section, too. Okay?"

"Just save me—" *The classifieds,* Nina almost said, but caught herself in the nick of time. She had not yet told her family about the layoffs. She would love not to tell them anything at all until she had a new job lined up.

Even at twelve, Zachary worried too much. Nina figured that came with the territory of being the man of the house before you'd shaved your first whisker. But when he worried, his asthma kicked in...and then *she* worried.

"Save the rest of the paper for me," Nina told her son, refraining from asking if he'd had to use his inhaler today.

"Okay. When's lunch?"

"I think it may be ready, so stick around."

Zach took his paper to the couch and sat down to read, neatly separating sections and placing them aside until he came to the sports. He was so much like her, Nina mused—calm, methodical.... Abruptly she amended her thought. No, he was the way she'd been *before* she'd gone secretary on her boss.

Deciding to leave the classifieds until she had some private time, she deposited her heavy bag by the door and halfheartedly followed the aromas to the kitchen.

Under her great grandmother's watchful eye, Isabella dusted a pan of *mandelbrodt* with cinnamon sugar.

"Now that smells wonderful." Nina reached over her daughter's shoulder to sample one of the long cookies.

Bubby's gnarled hand, made quick from years of baking and hand slapping, shot out to admonish her granddaughter. "Not so fast. You'll have soup first."

Nina exchanged smiles with her daughter. "Well, when you put it that way. Anything I can do?"

"Go sit," her grandmother directed, and gratefully Nina retreated to a small 1950s-style Formica-topped table that nestled near the window of their third-floor apartment. Feeling immeasurably tired, she watched her daughter and grandmother and thanked God for Bubby, five foot nothing, but with strength that couldn't be measured in inches and a love for family that made her seem mountainously large.

Bubby didn't live with them—she liked to keep her own apartment—but she babysat anytime Nina needed her, and she was a steady, loving influence in her great grandchildren's lives, as she'd always been in Nina's.

"Izzy dolly." Bubby put a hand on Isabella's shoulder. "This is a special lunch you made. Go change into something nice, very nice, so we can dine like civilized people."

The opportunity to wear one of her fancy dresses sent Isabella running happily to her room.

Bubby poured two mugs of coffee from the electric pot on the counter and stacked a plate with the warm *mandelbrodt*. Dressed cozily in dark blue polyester stretch pants and a matching blue sweatshirt that read If You Don't Like It, I Didn't Cook It, she ambled to the table with the skill of a career waitress. Nina knew better than to offend Bubby by offering to help.

"Huh, so I do get cookies before soup?" she asked, then looked down at her own clothing. Faded jeans and a beige cable-knit sweater with floppy sleeves were more suited to moving day than to the "civilized" family lunch Bubby requested. "Don't you want me to change my clothes, too?" Nina eyed the steaming mugs of caffeine and hoped the answer was no.

"Stay put," Bubby directed, setting everything down, then lowering herself to a chair with an exaggerated groan. "The weather in Chicago is not good for my bones. I should move to Orlando. Me and Mickey Mouse."

Nina had heard the I'm-moving-to-Florida threat too often to take it seriously. "The Wilkens Senior Center would be lost without your *rugelach*," she said, and Bubby nodded.

"True."

Deciding the cinnamon sugar would settle her stomach, Nina sampled one of the *mandelbrodt*. "Mmmm."

"What's wrong?"

Dunking the bitten tip of her cookie into the coffee, Nina cocked her head at her grandmother. "Nothing. It's delicious."

Impatiently, Bubby slapped a hand at the air. "Not the cookie." She leaned forward, sharp blue eyes narrowing. "You got something to tell me?"

So much for hoping the cinnamon would settle her stomach. Nina took her time pulling a napkin from the Lucite holder on the table and set her cookie neatly on top of the white square. "Well…offhand, I can't think of—"

"Ellie Berkowitz gets the Sunday paper. She likes the coupons. Today she read the business section. I don't know why." Bubby shrugged. "Maybe she wants to sleep with Morty Rosenfeld. He's a retired CEO, and she was always a floozy." Bubby took a sip of steaming coffee then waved a hand. "But that's not the point."

She leaned farther over the table, her aging bosom resting on the Formica. "The point is Ellie called here this morning, because she knew I'd be here, and she asks me, 'Rayzel, why didn't you tell me there were more layoffs at Hanson?'" Bubby jerked back as if struck. "Layoffs at Hanson! Who knew? Not me." She placed crooked fingers over her chest. "But they couldn't affect my Nina, or she would have told me. Besides, I said to Ellie, Nina is at the office right now to drop off some work she did over the weekend."

Nina frowned morosely at her coffee, her mind hopping from one barely plausible excuse to another. She needn't have bothered.

"Of course," Bubby continued, "I said all this before I knew that Ellie Berkowitz's niece, Carla, got a job at a new coffee store downtown—Some Like It Hot. Good for her."

"What does this have to—"

"I'm getting there. I'm old. Be a little patient, maybe." Bubby licked her dry lips. She looked her granddaughter in the eye. "Carla's son Anthony goes to school with Isaac—another thing I didn't know, and Carla called Ellie, because she recognized you walking down the street this morning. It looked like you were crying, she said. She was concerned. Some Like It Hot is right near your office." Bubby sat back in her chair, hands resting atop the table. "Carla read the paper, too."

Plowing fingers into her thick curls, Nina wagged her head then looked toward the kitchen door to make sure neither of her children was on the way in.

"I didn't want to worry you or the kids," she said softly. "I thought if I had a few job prospects when I told you, you wouldn't worry so much."

She must have sounded as miserable as she felt because Bubby turned immediately comforting. "Me worry? Who's worried?" She reached across the table to clutch Nina's hand. They sat in silence for several moments.

"I'm sorry you had to hear the news from Ellie Berkowitz," Nina murmured.

"Ah, she's such an old gossip." Leaning back in her chair, she looked around the kitchen. "How much did you say your rent was going up?"

Nina winced at the mere mention of the notice she'd received two weeks before. The older building they were in had been sold. The new owners planned to remodel the exterior and make other upgrades. The rent was going to jump a hundred dollars a month, effective on the first of the month—ten days away.

"It's the timing of this that stinks," Nina said, propping her head in her hand. "I had a little savings, but then Izzy needed a Girl Scout uniform and Isaac's music teacher said he needed a better violin to practice on."

Since the kids had been in kindergarten, Nina had been squirreling away just enough money each paycheck to buy a savings bond here, a savings bond there, always in their names and hers. She'd sworn to herself, though, that she would never dip into their savings for the household needs.

"I have some money," Bubby began, but Nina squeezed her hand to halt the offer.

"You're not touching your Social Security. You'll need it for your own rainy day. No," she said when Bubby opened her mouth to protest. "We're going to be okay. I have an excellent employment history, and I'm a hard worker. And I haven't looked in the Sunday paper yet. I bet just the right job is going to be in there." She smiled then raised her thumb to her lips and nibbled unconsciously on the cuticle.

"I thought David Hanson was such a nice man," Bubby said sadly, wagging her salt-and-pepper head. "He gave Isabella that cute bear."

"That was ten years ago." Nina pushed back her chair and leaned her head against the windowpane.

The day she'd had Izzy by C-section had also been the day she'd received her final divorce papers by mail. Nothing, not even flowers, had come from her ex, but a giant stuffed teddy bear had arrived from Hanson Media. When Nina had called to say thank-you, the temporary receptionist had told her that David Hanson himself had gone out on his lunch hour and brought the bear back with him. He'd been off on one of his many trips to the Far East when Nina returned to work, so she'd left a thank you note, which he'd never acknowledged. That had been the end of that, but he'd won a fan in Bubby for life.

"You'd think he could have found you another job in the office," Bubby insisted. "Maybe if he knew the situation—"

"I've already seen David Hanson," Nina said to squelch any thought that she might go see him again. "He knows how I feel." A careful understatement.

Bubby rose to stir her soup. "I suppose you never know about people," she said sadly. "And he even attends the Special Olympics every year."

"Yeah. Well." Nina wasn't entirely sure what that had to do with the layoffs, but she chose not to pursue it.

As she watched Bubby taste the soup and add a pinch of pepper, Nina tapped her unpolished fingernails on the Formica, knowing she was too antsy to sit still for lunch. Regardless of what she'd said about her ability to get a new job, she knew the market was tight and that even a few-week lapse of employment could be devastating given her rent increase. Worse, she would now have to pay for her family's health insurance out of her own pocket.

"Lunch is ready. I'll call the children." Bubby wiped her hands on her flowered apron.

Nina jumped from the chair. "I'll be right back."

"Where are you going?"

"To talk to Mr. Goldman."

Bubby scowled. "What for? He likes my chicken soup all of a sudden?"

Arthur Goldman was the manager of Nina's apartment building, and Bubby had never thought much of the man. He didn't keep the hallway clean enough in her opinion, and he smoked clove cigarettes in a nonsmoking building.

"I don't want him to come to lunch," Bubby said.

"I'm not asking him to come to lunch." Nina fished a rubber band out of the "everything" drawer and scraped her hair into a ponytail. "I'm going to explain my situation and ask him to talk to the new owners on our behalf or to give me their number. Then I'm going to remind him that we are stellar tenants, that stellar tenants are not easy to come by, and that I have never once complained about the stench his clove cigarettes leave in the hallway."

"You'd be better off talking to David Hanson. I bet

he sweeps his hallway!" Bubby called as Nina headed toward the door.

"I bet he hires someone to sweep his hallway," Nina tossed over her shoulder without breaking stride. "I doubt David Hanson would know which end of a broom to put on the floor, and I am absolutely certain he has better things to do than to concern himself with my problems. Or the problems of any of his *ex*-employees."

Entering the living room with Bubby at her heels, Nina assured herself that her son was still deeply engrossed in the sports section. She reached for the doorknob. "I'm going to buy myself a little leeway, and then I am going to blow the Hanson dust off my shoes and not look back." She paused briefly to meet Bubby's doubtful gaze. Despite her grandmother's brave claim, Nina could see worry fading the aging blue eyes.

She took her grandmother by the shoulders. "I've got you and the kids," she said quietly. "And you've got me. I refuse to worry. I've got smarts and I've got chutzpah."

Feeling stronger almost instantly with a simple change in attitude, she admonished herself for allowing someone—anyone—else's actions to frighten her. Hadn't she learned better over the years?

Standing as tall as her five-foot-three frame allowed, she opened the door and stepped into the hall. "I don't need anyone to rescue me," she reassured

Bubby, summoning her first genuine smile in the past three days, "least of all a corporate suit who, despite having laid off half his employees, will not miss a single meal at his favorite five-star feedlot, I am sure. Know what I mean?"

"I think I get the picture."

Nina jumped, literally jumped in the air, as she whirled around.

David Hanson stood in the hallway of her modest apartment building. Dressed in the designer clothes he wore, apparently, even on weekends, he frowned at the purple hat and scarf in his hands.

"You left these on your desk, Miss Baxter." He raised unreadable brown eyes. "As the day is chilly, and I'm about to be responsible for turning off your heat, I thought you might need them."

Chapter Two

While her family entertained David Hanson in their living room, Nina stood in her bathroom and wondered how long it would take for anyone to discover she'd climbed out the window.

Immediately upon seeing David in the hallway, Bubby had pulled him into the apartment, sat him on the couch next to Zach and shooed Nina toward the bedrooms.

"Go! See what's taking Izzy so long," her grandmother had said in an overly hearty voice and with an overly cheerful smile. *Put on some lipstick,* Bubby had mouthed to Nina as she'd shoved her down the hallway.

Turning to gaze into the mirror, Nina shook her head at her sad reflection. She'd been grateful for any excuse to escape David's serious, censorious gaze, but lipstick, she feared, would not cure what ailed her.

Leaning toward the glass her children routinely splattered with toothpaste, she shook her head. Could she have been any more of a doofus today?

Probably not, because according to her calculations, she had just run out of feet to put in her mouth.

Morose but dutiful, she plucked a lipstick from the basket of makeup she kept on the sink. She uncapped the tube and raised it to her lips, then halted. She wore no other makeup. Scooped into a ponytail, her curly hair looked like a profusion of yellow ribbons exploding behind her head. No wonder David Hanson hadn't immediately recognized her in the office.

For work she always, but always, tamed her flyaway kinks into a twist or bun or French braid. And she'd always dressed conservatively, in suits and blouses. Neat. Respectful. Appropriate.

Recapping the lipstick, she dropped it into the basket. Why bother? No matter what Bubby thought, an attractive appearance was not going to help her get her job back. And Shell-Pink Long-Lasting Lipwear would not erase David Hanson's memory of how she had behaved today.

All she could do now was go to the living room, thank Mr. Hanson for very kindly returning her hat and scarf, and bid the man a permanent if not overly fond farewell.

Snapping off the light, she headed down the hall. Before she reached the living room, she heard Bubby say, "Not too many *mandelbrodt* now, David. You'll spoil your appetite."

Oh, dear Lord, no. Bubby couldn't have…she wouldn't have…. Nina practically sprinted the remaining steps to where her children and grandmother were entertaining a bemused David Hanson. He held a coffee mug in one hand, a cookie in the other. Busy chewing, he looked up as she skidded to a stop.

"David is having lunch with us," Bubby announced.

"No!" Nina blurted. She glanced frankly at David. "I appreciate your bringing my things. I do." Offering what she hoped was an ironic and understanding smile, she said, "You don't have to have lunch with us."

It took David a moment to swallow his cookie. Another moment to respond, "But I'm hungry."

He looked dead serious.

"Can I show David my room?" Zach turned toward his mother. "He likes chemistry sets."

"And I want to show him Jo-Jo," Izzy said, referring to her giant bear. Dressed in her fanciest pink dress, Izzy sat close to David on the couch. "Bubby said he gave me Jo-Jo when I was born."

"He" looked at Nina with an expression she could not read. Four sets of eyes were trained on her, each anticipating her response. She couldn't believe David

Hanson wanted to eat chicken soup with a laid-off employee, her obviously besotted grandmother and her hungry-for-any-male-attention children.

Seated rather stiffly between Izzy and Zach, holding his cookie and drink at right angles to his body, he resembled a big, gangly new kid in school—willing to be included, but not quite certain what to do with the people around him.

What was he up to? Nina felt like she was slogging her way through some weird dream, the kind where you tried to speak, but no sound emerged.

"Kinderle," Bubby said, motioning for Isabella and Zach to come to her. "Help me set the table. We'll call Mr. Hanson and your mother when we're ready."

She ushered the children into the kitchen, turning back to Nina and gesturing madly for her to take her ponytail down. David, fortunately, was still looking at Nina and missed the fervent signal.

When her children and Bubby were safely in the kitchen, Nina looked at her ex-boss and shook her head ineloquently. "I have no idea what to say." Spreading her hands, she shrugged. "You have seen me at my absolute worst today. I'm very embarrassed." A wry laugh warbled from her chest. "Humiliated, really. I can't imagine that you honestly want to have lunch with us. I realize you're trying to be polite…which is more than I can say for myself today…but it's not—"

David stood. "I'm not polite." He set his mug on the coffee table and held up the biscotti-shaped *mandelbrodt*. "I like this. Your grandmother is a good baker. You have a nice family."

The best Nina could offer was a bemused frown. "Okay."

"And I am hungry." Without the slightest change in his sober expression, he added, "I missed lunch. My favorite five-star feedlot is closed Sundays."

Nina felt her face flush, a lovely complement, she was sure, to her firecracker hair.

"You fired me," she said, unwilling to remain on the defensive. That had to be a good excuse for feeling testy.

David's chest rose and fell on a long breath. "There were layoffs," he corrected. "You got caught in them and for that I am sorry. The board hired an external accountant to thoroughly examine Hanson's finances, and it was determined quickly that the company cannot support a full staff at present and survive."

David felt some of the tension leave his body. There. He had said exactly what he had come to say. When he'd recognized Nina in the office and realized she was one of the layoffs, he'd felt a stab of highly unprofessional guilt. In truth, he felt guilty for every one of the layoffs. Hell, lately he'd been feeling guilty simply for bearing his last name.

As CEO of Hanson Media, his brother, George, had made mistakes that caused suffering throughout the company and cost Hanson its reputation. David had been working daily—and often nightly—to repair the damage. He'd been in Tokyo recently, solidifying relationships with Hanson's existing Asian partners.

He'd arrived home last night and was still exhausted and jet-lagged today. He'd missed the board meeting at which the layoffs had been finalized. He hadn't had time yet to scan the list of dismissed employees. Or perhaps he'd been avoiding that task.

In any case, David was glad he was here, explaining the situation more clearly to Nina Baxter, helping her to understand.

"Layoffs aren't personal," he said in a tone he hoped was reassuring, soothing. He wanted to smooth the frown from her face. "I realize it's difficult not to feel rejected—"

"Rejected?" she interrupted, her big blue eyes blinking several times, rapidly. She shook her head like a swimmer clearing water from her ears. "You think I feel 'rejected'? Mr. Hanson, I'm not upset because you didn't ask me to the prom. I'm the head of a one-income household." She tapped her chest. "Me. All alone. I couldn't care less about getting my feelings hurt. I am worried about my children's ability to grow to the age of thirteen on a steady diet of boiled potatoes and boxed macaroni with fluorescent cheese."

On a roll, she barely inhaled before continuing. "I

know the company is in trouble, but I didn't cause that trouble. Janet Daitch from sales has been with Hanson for eight years. She's a grandmother. She was hoping this would be her last job. She didn't cause any of the problems, either. And Joe from the mailroom?" She raised a hand in a gesture that said *ditto.* "Maybe the board of directors should call another meeting to determine how *they* could help ease some of the burden. Maybe the executives should, too. Last week I was told to make reservations at Season's Restaurant for an *informal* dinner meeting."

She didn't have to say any more. Season's was one of the most expensive restaurants in the city.

David felt the tension seep—no, flood—back into his shoulders, neck and head. He was going to be an old man before his time, thanks to his careless brother and the burdens George had bequeathed to the family.

"I can't mandate the location of business meetings," David said carefully, taking one last shot at conciliation. "But I'll mention your point at the next board meeting. And I will see to it that the severance packages are dispersed promptly."

"What severance packages?" Nina Baxter looked blatantly disgusted with him. "Janet Daitch got two extra-strength Excedrin from the head of HR when he broke the bad news, but from what I've heard, that's the most anyone was offered." Folding her arms, she stared at him in challenge. "We stood by your company, Mr. Hanson, when you were in trouble. We believed in you. Well, now we're in trouble. And no matter how you put it or how reasonable the layoffs were, it still…sucks."

An alien sense of failure stabbed David's gut. He was head of public relations; he ought to be able to fix this.

"Lunch is ready!" Her grandmother's voice carried from the kitchen. A moment later the woman he'd met only as "Bubby" poked her head around the corner. "Come, children. It's only soup and a few latkes I pulled from Nina's freezer, but the latkes are to die for. Such a cook, this granddaughter of mine. Come. Eat while it's hot."

David glanced at Nina. She wanted him to leave. Nothing could have been plainer. The situation was awkward and unsatisfying for them both. He had only words with which to appease her, and she didn't need words.

Regretfully, David geared himself up to disappoint a good-hearted seventy-year-old woman. "It's been a pleasure meeting you…" he began. With that brief opening, he saw Nina's shoulders drop in relief. She knew he was about to beg off and didn't bother to mask her pleasure.

Returning his attention to her grandmother, he continued. "And I'm looking forward to trying your soup, Bubby." Closing the distance between him and Nina, he held out an arm. "Shall we?"

Nina's brows hitched almost comically then swooped into a scowl. Pretending not to notice, David smiled.

Bubby clucked her approval from the kitchen. The approval, however, quickly turned to exasperation when Nina failed to move. "Nina dolly, a man holds out his arm, he's not asking if you want to hang your hat. So, come on, already."

She turned and disappeared into the kitchen, leaving Nina to stare warily at her former employer. "I haven't told my children yet that I was fired—"

"Laid off."

She snapped her fingers. "Yes, laid off. And I will explain that difference to them. Right after I sell their computer for lunch money. Now, as I was saying, I haven't told them I was fired. I will do that in my own way and in my own time. Please do not blow it for me. My children tend to worry. If Isaac has to use his inhaler today because you slip up, Mr. Hanson, I will escort you out of my home even if you have one of Bubby's matzo balls hanging halfway out of your mouth."

David grinned. "Miss Baxter, your way with words is exceeded only by your hospitality." He raised his arm a bit higher. Nina ignored the offer, but walked by his side toward the kitchen. "What's wrong with Isaac?" he asked.

"Nothing's wrong with him. He has asthma."

"Serious?"

"Asthma is never a joke." She'd already lowered her voice, but now she dropped it to a near whisper. "He doesn't like us to discuss it. Please don't mention that, either."

He frowned but said nothing else. As they were about to step into the kitchen, he took her hand despite her protest and tucked it into his arm. "Your grandmother will like this," he said, holding her firmly when she tried to pull back. "And I like making elderly people happy. My karma needs a good deed today, so humor me."

Nina endured lunch. That was really the most she could say for her lack of contribution to an otherwise lighthearted meal.

Her children kept David entertained with accounts of their experiences in music and dance classes and the field trips they'd taken during the current school year. At first, David responded to her children's breathless chattering as if he were viewing a foreign species. Then he began to relax…and smile. He laughed outright at Zach's impression of his teacher's dismay when a papier-mâché volcano prematurely exploded during a school science fair, and he told Isabella that he thought she must be a very good dancer because he could see that she looked like Julie Kent. When Isabella asked who Julia Kent was, David told her that Ms. Kent was the greatest ballerina dancing today and asked if Izzy had ever attended a professional ballet.

Nina wanted to ask if he knew what tickets to the ballet cost these days, but she bit her tongue and just listened. He was good with the kids—easily admitted what he didn't know (had not a clue about Maroon 5 or Captain Underpants)—and didn't talk down to them. But his very presence at her table underscored the chasm between his world and hers. He'd never had matzo balls before, he ate his latkes with a knife and fork, and he chewed *and swallowed* before speaking. Dining mostly with children for the past twelve years, Nina had forgotten that was an option.

After lunch, Zach and Izzy dragged David to see their room. Nina immersed herself immediately in cleaning up.

"I like him," Bubby said without preamble as she joined Nina at the sink, picking up a towel to dry the dishes Nina washed.

Hoping to avoid conversation about David at least until she could gather her thoughts, Nina urged, "Bubby, have a cup of tea and relax in the living room. You did the cooking." She reached for the towel, but her grandmother whipped it away.

"I relax better in the kitchen." Wiping off a soup bowl, Bubby eyed Nina shrewdly. "You don't want me to talk about him, but why not? He didn't want to fire anybody. I can tell."

"You can?" She felt her lips curl into an unflattering twist. "How's that?"

"He looked at your plate when you weren't watching. It bothered him you didn't eat."

Nina released a hoot of laughter. "That's how you know he didn't want to lay off half his staff? Because he was eyeing my matzo balls? Maybe he just wanted more food. The Hansons love acquisitions."

"I don't know what's this 'acquisitions,' but I know what's guilt, and that man feels terrible."

"I don't think so."

"Ah, maybe you're right." The gray head wagged sadly. "Maybe he doesn't care. But then why does he come here? Why does he have lunch with an old woman and two children and his secretary?"

"I was never 'his' secretary," Nina corrected. "Except for a very brief time when his AA was out of the office and I filled in. Really, I've never had that much to do with him other than working in his department."

Bubby raised sparse but eloquent brows. "So? Even more strange that he should care enough to come talk to you."

"All right, he feels guilty. Big whoop. A flash of guilt does not make him Nelson Mandela. David Hanson is part of the problem, he is not the solution, so don't romanticize him. He didn't ride here on a white horse to save the day." Scrubbing the pan Bubby had used to reheat the latkes, Nina muttered, "More likely he double-parked his Porsche."

"Actually I drive a reconditioned Mustang that

belonged to one of my uncles. It was a college-graduation present. I still love it."

The latke pan clattered into the sink as Nina whirled. David filled the kitchen entrance. "How much did you hear this time?" she demanded.

"Not much." When she scowled doubtfully, he raised his right hand. "Honest, Your Honor."

His eyes glinted with deprecating humor, but Nina got the point: She was judging him, had been judging him all day. And that was strange for her, really, because she'd always liked the Hansons. She'd never before begrudged them their wealth. Or felt sorry for herself. She shook her head.

"Oy." Bubby bent side to side from the waist. "My aching back. Standing on hard linoleum is not so good for me anymore."

Nina reached for her arm. "Here, come sit at the table."

"No." Bubby edged away. "You know me. I can't relax in a kitchen." Heading for the living room, she handed David her dish towel. "Here. You dry. You don't mind? I'll sit on the sofa and put my feet up. And watch a little TV. I'll turn the sound up. I don't hear a thing when the sound is up."

David smiled as he watched her go, then, dish towel at the ready, he approached the sink and Nina.

She shook her head. "You do not have to—"

David's placed two fingers on Nina's lips. "Why bother?"

His smile was ironic, his brown eyes warm as they watched her. She'd never thought of David Hanson as warm before.

Immobilized by the unfamiliar and unexpected contact, Nina couldn't recall ever seeing him touch anyone at the office, not even at the company parties. His late brother, George, had been the back slapper, the inveterate shoulder patter. David was the head of public relations, but he was no schmoozer.

Slowly he lowered his fingers. "Hand me a plate, Miss Baxter. We'll get this show on the road."

Nina did as he asked. It was easier than arguing, and perhaps that was his intention, too: Get the job done and go. She handed him a bread dish, a soup bowl, a water glass.

And discovered that he didn't know squat about doing dishes.

He took too much care, polishing them as if he were waxing an automobile. She had to slow down the rinsing considerably. No one at the office could speak knowledgeably about his personal life, so all she knew came from the bits her grandmother had read in the Lifestyle pages. He was single, dated socialites, lived downtown. And obviously had a housekeeper.

"You don't do this much, do you?" For the first time since he'd arrived, she felt a bubble of humor. "That's not a judgment," she hastened to add when he glanced up and frowned. "I'm just asking, because you're very…diligent."

David arched a brow. "Dead giveaway?"

Nina nodded. "Pretty much. You can't be overly concerned about water spots when you don't have a dishwasher and you serve three meals a day. You'd never get out of the kitchen."

He looked ruefully at the plate he'd been polishing then at bowls and glasses waiting to be dried and the pot that hadn't even been washed. "You're going to do this again tonight?"

"Gotta clean 'em if you want to eat off 'em."

"And on workdays?"

"Well, then it's two meals a day." She almost restated that in the past tense, but decided to give him a break. "Do you eat any meals at home?"

Reaching for a new plate, he slid her a look. "A few. Not many. Is that a strike?"

"A strike? Against you? No." She shrugged. "I mean, it's not my business, anyway." After a moment, she grew wistful. "Although truthfully, I suppose that if anything, I envy you. I'd love to eat out more. Just put in our orders and send the plates back when we're done."

He accepted another bowl from her. "And where would you eat, Miss Baxter? If you could eat out every night?"

She smiled. "Good question. When we do go out, I usually choose a place I know the kids will like, so that means burritos for Isabella and burgers for Zach. But even that's a treat if I don't have to cook."

David was quiet after that, so they washed and dried—more quickly—in companionable silence. Nina insisted on putting everything away on her own, so when the last cup was clean, David folded his towel and hung it neatly over the sink. It was almost two o'clock.

"I'd better get back to the office," he said, his gaze on her but his mind someplace else. She could see the moody thoughtfulness that had crept in on him. He seemed distant and distracted: the remote Mr. Hanson she was used to seeing at the office.

"Do you usually work on Sundays?" she asked.

"No, not usually." His lips curved briefly. "Not *often*. But Hanson isn't experiencing 'usual' circumstances." He focused on her more closely. "You know that when my brother died, he left the business with unusual debts. And you were present for the Internet screwup last month."

Nina nodded. The Hanson Media Group Web site had been hijacked, and for twenty-four hours every visitor who had attempted to log on to Hanson's new interactive Web zine for kids had been mistakenly directed to a porn site. "My son was one of the visitors to the site that day."

David's brows shot up. "Zach?" He pressed a hand to his eyes and swore beneath his breath. "I didn't know that. I'm sorry."

It was one of the most sincere and regret-filled apologies Nina had ever heard. Hanson Media's reputation had been hit hard by the mix-up, and Nina knew that as head of public relations for the company, David must have been dancing as fast as he could to repair the damage. At the office, however, the stress rarely showed. Now, looking at the lines around David's tight mouth, she actually felt concerned by the stress she saw him carrying.

"Zach wasn't overly damaged by the experience," she said, injecting a note of wry humor into her voice. "In fact I'd say it was a rite of passage. And it forced that conversation I'd been meaning to have about hormones and teenage boys."

Lowering his hand, he looked at her gratefully. "You ought to be a spin doctor. I'm sorry you had to have that worry with your son."

His brown eyes grew more troubled. "A week ago we received notice that one of the major charities to which we contribute has 'grave concerns' about accepting our most recent donation. We believe that if they publicly sever ties, the damage to our reputation could be irreparable. It takes time to rebuild public trust, and time isn't something we have. We're walking a financial tightrope." His expression asked her to appreciate the import of what he was telling her. "None of the other…released employees has been given this information."

Because, Nina realized, if the information was leaked before David had the chance to ease the charity's concerns, the public damage would be a done deal. Not a bad way to wreak revenge on the company that had "released" you.

"I appreciate your telling me," she said. "It won't go any further."

He nodded. "It's time for me to go, I think. Thank you for sharing your family with me. I like them."

Aw, crud. Nina had been hoping to hang on to her resentment at least a little while longer, but he was making it darn hard. With the death of his brother, David had become the senior Hanson, the head of a Chicago dynasty. He was forty-four, well traveled, sophisticated. But his somber sincerity—and the humility with which he'd uttered the last sentence—made him seem more endearingly awkward than suave.

"Well, I think it's safe to say they like you, too."

They stood uncomfortably a moment, aware that neither of them had mentioned liking the other. David broke the lingering silence. "Goodbye, Nina."

His farewell held the ring of finality. Which was appropriate, Nina thought, absolutely appropriate. The truth was they didn't have a reason to see each other again and were unlikely to meet by chance—unless he had a sudden urge to watch a middle-school talent show or she was invited to the Oak Park Country Club.

"Goodbye, Mr. Hanson. Best of luck."

She thought he winced slightly, but recovered before saying, "You, too."

He headed for the kitchen's arched entrance then

stopped and turned. "By the way, where were you headed when I showed up at your door?"

Nina had to concentrate for a moment. "Oh! I was going to see the building manager. Our rent is going up next month, and I wanted to…"

Her voice trailed away when David's brow furrowed. Lord, she did not want to sound any more desperate than she had already today. In over a decade of fending mostly for herself, she'd learned to present a confident front. And she finally believed Bubby was right: David Hanson was a man plagued by his responsibilities. His conscience didn't need the weight of her burdens as well.

Backpedaling, she assured him, "The rent increase is no big deal. That was only my *excuse* to go see him, because…" She had no idea what she was going to say, hesitated and watched David's frown drop lower. "Because…" *Dang it!* Lying was not her forte. "I…have…a crush…on him. The building manager." She laughed. "Go figure."

She ushered David out of the kitchen and toward the front door.

"Bubby! Kids! Come say goodbye to Mr. Hanson!" she called, glad for the first time today that her family doted on him. In a matter of seconds, they claimed David's attention. The general consensus was that they didn't want him to leave, but after a few fawning moments, they allowed him to open the door and wedge out.

Saying her final goodbye before her children yanked off his arm in an attempt to pull him back into the apartment, Nina closed the door and sagged against it. *Thank heavens that was over.*

"Can we come to your office to see David? He's nice!" Izzy jumped up and down.

"I want to invite David to my violin recital." Zach was more calm than his sister, but equally enthusiastic.

"So what's this about the building manager?" Bubby stood with her arms crossed, her countenance unsmiling.

Nina remained where she was, back to the door, one hand on the knob. *There were days,* she thought, *that should have ended at dawn.*

She looked at her son. "Where's the paper?"

Chapter Three

David's jaw remained clenched as he descended the stairs leading to the foyer of Nina's apartment building. He'd spent an interesting afternoon. *Why* he had chosen to have lunch with Nina's family despite his hostess's obvious reluctance remained a mystery to him.

Or maybe it wasn't so mysterious.

She intrigued him. Nina Baxter had turned out to be a fascinating blend of hyper-responsible and Kewpie-doll charming, even when she was trying to insult him behind his back. David felt guilty about her job loss and concerned for her and her family's future. When he returned to the office, he intended to review the employee records and to attempt to work out some sort of severance package. He'd been in Asia during the last board meeting; call him a fool, but he'd had no idea that severance packages had been disregarded.

Nina Baxter, with her shock of blond curls, her emotion-filled blue eyes and her outspoken voice of the people, had wreaked havoc on his peace of mind. And that last comment, about the building manager...

"Has nothing to do with the layoffs and is none of your damned business," David muttered as he stepped off the last stair.

He had made it a policy never to nurture an attraction toward anyone with whom he had a work relationship.

Or toward anyone who had children.

Or who looked like the type to carve Halloween pumpkins and invite him to meet her family over the holidays.

If he'd ever gone on one of those bachelor TV shows he'd have failed miserably. He was a dyed-in-the-wool realist, actually got heartburn when he heard people say they'd fallen in love at first sight.

David enjoyed physical attraction, he enjoyed women, but those feelings were transitory. They could be managed. If a couple decided to marry, they should do so, he believed, only because they both supported the institution of marriage and believed it would enhance their lives. Not because of transient feelings, either physical or emotional.

Wishing he'd brought his coat from the office, rather than opting for only his sport jacket, David prepared to face the punishing Chicago wind, which had kicked in considerably since he'd left work. He'd come here on the train and planned to return the same way. He'd work a couple more hours then head home to get ready for a charity function that he hoped would help Hanson Media Group's reputation. The company had to show that it was still functional, still able to give.

Though not, apparently, to its own employees.

Chewing on that thought, David missed the other person in the lobby until he heard a phlegmy cough.

"Blowing like a sonovabitch."

A stout man, almost bald save for a rim of artificially dark hair that circled three-quarters of his head like a laurel wreath, stood at the glass-walled entrance and pointed with a cigarette held between his thumb and index finger.

"I beg your pardon?" David asked.

"The wind," the other man clarified. "Bastard's getting worse, not better. I gotta replace a window screen in 102. Gonna freeze my keister off." He dragged on the cigarette and shook his head. "I shoulda moved to Philly when I had the chance."

David focused on the man's comment about the window. "You're a handyman?"

"Yeah. Handyman, collection agent, and the building shrink, too. Apartment managers—we're like barbers. Everyone wants to tell you their troubles."

"You're the manager of this building?"

"Yeah."

"Is there a second manager?"

Instantly the man's unibrow swooped. "Why? You got a complaint?"

"Not at all." David looked at the man upon whom Nina supposedly had a crush and decided that no, he had no complaints at all. "Actually, the building is very well-kept," he commented. "I was wondering how one manager alone could be responsible." Perhaps he'd spent too many years in public relations, but the fib flowed smoothly. And had the desired effect.

The round, stubbled face bobbed in satisfaction. Nina Baxter's apartment manager stabbed a thick thumb at his chest. "I'm responsible, all right. Only me. When I'm on the job, one super's all you need."

Puffed with pride, the burly man pointed his cigarette in David's direction. "You looking for a place to hang your hat?"

David began to reply in the negative then thought better of it. Nina Baxter had lied about having a crush on her super. He didn't know her well, but he knew that. Now the question was, why had she done it?

"I may be interested," he said. "What can you tell me about the apartments? Start with price."

* * *

On Monday morning, Nina sat on the floor in her living room, Sunday classifieds spread out over her coffee table, a red felt-tip marker in hand and the cordless phone lying by her side with only a small charge left to give it life.

She knew just how the depleted phone felt.

Stretching backward over the couch, she heard something in her body pop, but was too tired to pinpoint exactly what or where. It was 11:00 a.m.; she'd been sitting here circling help-wanted ads and making phone calls since she'd dropped the kids off at school. A mug of bitterly strong coffee sat on the table, too, because she'd only had two hours of sleep…*maybe* two hours…the night before. Isaac had been up twice needing to use his inhaler.

Watching her son struggle to find a useful breath had always terrified her beyond anything else she could imagine. Last night was the worst. Without a job, without the knowledge that she could take care of her family, Isaac's fight for air on Sunday scared her more than ever before. She'd wanted to rush him to the emergency room immediately, before knowing whether the inhaler would help. She'd wanted to phone the paramedics and to ask one of the EMTs to hold her hand.

In the end, she'd kept her cool—outwardly at least. After a decade of parenting alone, she had come to believe that was sometimes enough. She'd dealt with Isaac the way his doctors had instructed, the way she had too many times before, and she'd held him in the aftermath, the two of them quietly reassuring each other that everything was okay and then reassuring Izzy, who had woken up at the height of it all.

Because her children had school the next today, Nina had lured them back to sleep with the promise of chocolate-chip waffles in the morning. She'd stayed awake, though, listening for the sound of Isaac's breathing, and creeping to their door several times in the dark early morning, not falling asleep until exhaustion overcame maternal fear…which happened as it usually did, about five minutes before her alarm went off in the morning.

Now, as she struggled to stay awake despite the infusion of caffeine, she wondered why she didn't just get back into bed till the kids came home. Scouring the want ads wasn't getting her anywhere. Most of the office positions available were part time; the full-time jobs with benefits often required experience in fields that were unfamiliar to her. With multitudes of applicants for the better positions, employers could afford to be choosy.

She felt defeated, and it wasn't even mid-day.

And then the phone rang.

"I have a proposition for you."

He did not have to add "Miss Baxter" for Nina to identify the voice. Measured, cultured, as rich as brandy, David Hanson's voice sent a shiver of feminine response down Nina's back and put a buzz of foreboding in her belly.

"What kind of proposition?"

"Are you busy?" he asked.

"Now?"

David paused, and Nina pictured him checking his watch. "In thirty minutes. I'll have an hour free then. I can come to you, or we can meet somewhere. Have you had lunch?"

"It's only eleven." She hadn't yet managed breakfast. There was a cold chocolate-chip waffle with her name on it in the kitchen.

"Hmm. How about if we meet at twelve then? I can work that out. If I head to your neck of the woods, can you direct us to a good lunch place?"

"I haven't said I'm going to meet you," Nina replied baldly, then almost added *sir*. She'd never been anything but unfailingly polite to her bosses. Reminding herself that the events of the weekend had changed the status quo, she said, "Why do you want to see me?"

There was a brief pause. "Have you found a new job yet?"

"No. But I just sat down to look at the paper," she lied.

"Maybe you could look at it after lunch…that is, if you don't like what I have to say. You may not need to look at the classifieds at all, Miss Baxter." She heard the sound of papers being shuffled…then a muffled voice…and his response as he held the phone away from himself. "I've got to go. Pick a lunch spot near your apartment."

He waited for her response, and Nina hesitated only briefly. "I'll meet you near your office. In front of Some Like It Hot." Give Mrs. Berkowitz's niece Carla a thrill.

David rang off without further ado, obviously needing to get back to business. Nina looked at her phone, pressed End and remained where she was a considerable time, staring at nothing. Her mind hopped along several scenarios, all of which featured her being rehired at Hanson Media. She was sure that was why David had called and why he wanted to meet, and she began to feel immense relief, along with a healthy measure of vindication.

David Hanson, business mogul, must have been moved by something she had said yesterday when she had been too distraught to be tactical. Perhaps he planned to rehire a number of the other laid-off staffers as well. The thought was invigorating.

Abandoning the newspaper and the red marker, Nina sprang from the floor with more energy than she'd had in three days. She had an hour to shower, dress and get downtown. Like on any other workday.

Even with the short notice, Nina was in front of Some Like It Hot with several minutes to spare. David was waiting for her.

"Miss Baxter," he nodded politely in greeting. "Thank you for meeting me."

As always, the combination of his suave good looks and his almost nerdy formality bemused her.

"Are you hungry yet?" he asked.

With the chocolate chip waffle growing stale on her kitchen counter, Nina was aware of a growl deep in her belly. She had a strong aversion, however, to spending the money in her wallet on lunch at an over-priced Hanson-style restaurant. The mother in her would rather bring home a treat for her kids. Also the worrywart in her said, *He hasn't given you your job back yet. Celebrate after you're sitting behind your desk.*

Staring at the lapel of David's elegant gray suit, she said, "Something light, maybe. A sandwich?" She hitched a thumb over her shoulder. "There's a deli down the block…."

"Roseman's? I love that place." He put a hand beneath her elbow. "Let's go."

Surprised that David knew about, much less loved, the no-frills deli that had never even bothered to cover their subfloor, she fell into step beside him. They walked the block to the restaurant without small talk, which Nina thought was rather nice and rather awkward at the same time.

At a few minutes before noon, the deli was crowded, but mostly with the take-out crowd. Nina's eyes darted in several directions as she realized they could easily bump into someone from the office—someone whose brows were sure to rise when they saw David with a recently laid-off female employee, someone with whom he'd never had much personal contact in the office.

David, however, seemed unconcerned by the possibility, or perhaps he hadn't considered it, which seemed odd for a man who ran a public-relations department. Nina would have thought that appearances would be uppermost in his mind, but he smiled as the hostess greeted them, put a hand on the small of Nina's back and didn't demur when the young woman led them to a table in the center of the room.

When the hostess left, he picked up his menu and scanned it as if there were nothing more pressing in this moment than deciding between the "mile-high" turkey and the pastrami on rye.

"What do you like when you come here?" he asked.

Nina leaned toward him. "I like the table near the kitchen."

David looked up, quizzical. "Really?" He glanced over. "Seems cramped." Sending her a dazzling smile that made her forget for a moment why they were there, he shrugged. "It's empty. We'd better grab it now."

She put a hand on his arm as he started to rise. "My point is we could run into someone from the office. What will people think if they see us here, knowing I was laid off, and then I show up at my desk again?" She still didn't know *for sure* that he was planning to rehire anybody else. "It could look—"

The arrival of the waitress, who clearly wanted to get their orders in before the lunch rush began in earnest, temporarily halted their conversation, but Nina was glad she'd addressed the concern out loud.

David chose the mile-high turkey sandwich with a side of potato pancakes. "I'm addicted since yesterday," he admitted, and Nina put in her considerably smaller order: a dinner salad with a scoop of tuna. David frowned at her choice. "She'll take an order of pancakes, too."

Taken aback, Nina shook her head at him. "No, I won't." Turning, she shook her head at the waitress. "No, I won't."

David frowned. "Hmm." He glanced again at the menu. "One of the dough things then, with the potatoes inside. What are those called? Knishes?" He smiled at the young woman whose pencil was poised above her check pad. "We'll have a potato *nish*, too," he ordered, mispronouncing the word.

"It's *k-nish*," Nina corrected, smiling when he pursed his lips and frowned at the menu. He wore the same expression Zach did when studying for a spelling test.

Vulnerable, she thought, surprised the word popped into her mind, but the truth was that the dignified, distant David Hanson she knew from work seemed almost endearingly vulnerable when he was up-close and personal. Then again, maybe she only thought that because she'd insulted him so much.

She handed her plastic menu to the waitress. "Kibosh on the knish."

Flipping easily from eraser to pencil tip, the waitress adjusted the check and beat a hasty retreat.

David took a sip of water. "Not a potato eater, not hungry or you prefer to order for yourself?"

"The latter."

He nodded, set his water glass back on the table. "I'll make a mental note."

There was no further talk of changing tables, and they settled into the utilitarian wooden chairs.

David rested one wrist on the table. "Now where were we? Oh, yes. You were worried about running into someone from the office." He shook his head. "That's not an issue, I'm afraid. Hanson Media isn't going to be able to re-staff for some time."

Nina was so attached to the notion that he was rehiring her and so hopeful that he would rehire at least a few of her co-workers that she didn't immediately grasp what he was telling her. "Hanson isn't rehiring any *other* people, you mean?"

David pursed his lips. His dark eyes grew concerned. "Hanson isn't rehiring at all." He rubbed his temple. "I should have explained the situation better when we were on the phone."

Nina's heart sank. She was not returning to her favorite desk and her ergonomically correct chair? "Then why am I here?" she asked. *Spending eight dollars for iceberg lettuce and a can of tuna when my family is about to lose the roof over their heads?* She looked around for the waitress, so she could cancel her order. Or change it to hot tea and two aspirin.

"You're here, Miss Baxter, because although our current circumstances do preclude rehiring at the office, I find that those same circumstances require me to do a great deal of work from my home. I can't ask my secretary to take on the extra load. So I would benefit from a personal assistant who would work out of my house." He steadily held her gaze. "Are you interested?"

"You want me to be your in-home personal secretary?"

"There wouldn't be a great deal of computer work, other than keeping track of schedules and budgets involving work-related expenditures. I'll handle my personal accounts. Your job description would include coordinating the details of business parties and attending the functions as well, or at least some of them. I'd also ask you to run errands and coordinate the household staff—things I would not ask you to take on if we were in the office."

He let her absorb that info while he studied a bowl of pickle slices. "Do you think these are sweet and dill or all dill?"

"All dill."

"Hmm." He started to dig in then lifted the bowl to her even though it had been sitting on the table between them since they sat down. "Would you like one?"

Mechanically she took a pickle slice, but while he bit into his, she merely stared at hers.

"Is this a pity thing?" she asked. "Or a guilt thing?" She held up a hand before he could answer. "Never mind. I'm not sure I want to know."

She didn't want a reason to turn him down before he told her all the details. A job was a job, after all, and she was desperate. The longer she waited in the hope of finding something she really liked, the harder it would be ever to recoup her losses. As long as he wasn't asking her to do anything illegal or morally unsound, did it matter whether she worked in a home office or a high-rise building?

"You're wondering if I really need an assistant," David remarked, wiping his hands on a napkin. "Miss Baxter, I am by no means broke, but given Hanson Media's current state, neither can I afford to throw money away. I need a personal assistant and you need a job. You have a good work record, I like you—when you're not insulting me or throwing desert flora around my office—and I like your family. That seems a good start to our association. Assuming, of course, your feelings toward me have…gentled somewhat since yesterday? I don't want to be brained by a cactus when I least expect it."

He made the comment with a remarkably straight

face. And certainly, in light of yesterday, the comment was reasonable enough. Nina felt a blush infuse her cheeks, nonetheless. Something about David's formality actually made his question regarding her feelings seem more intimate.

"You know, when you talk like that you sound like Rex Harrison." Nina's hands flew to cover her mouth. She was never rude. Ordinarily, she never even came close to risking rudeness. "I'm sorry! I shouldn't have said that. I just meant…" She shook her head, not sure, really, what she meant.

David's brow puckered. "Hmm. I always liked Rex Harrison. If you hadn't apologized, I'd have thought you were complimenting me."

"No." Her eyes widened in dismay. "Oh! I mean—"

"Never mind. I'm not sure my ego can weather the explanation." He paused while the waitress set salad and sandwich in front of them.

"I'll be back with the latkes," she said and zoomed off. David looked at Nina for clarification. "Latkes. These are the potato pancakes, right?"

"Yes." Nina looked at her lunch, but felt too guilty to think it looked appetizing.

"Ah." He removed the top slice of bread from his sandwich and reached for the mustard. "Did you grow up on this type of food, Miss Baxter?" His tone indicated that he was prepared to forgive her faux pas.

"Yes. And on Rex Harrison films," she said. "I always liked him very much, just for the record."

He smiled, not broadly, but with irony. "But you thought he was stiff? Formal?"

"No. Not exactly." He didn't believe her at this point, of course, so she admitted, "I thought he was…remote. You know, kind of set apart from other people." David's pensive expression made him look vulnerable again, so she added hastily, "But in a good way!"

David winced. "Uh-oh. You've gone from insulting me to placating me. The situation must be worse than I realized." Replacing the bread he'd spread with mustard, he picked up half his sandwich. "Tell me, does this…remoteness…impact my effectiveness at the office?"

"No! Not at all." She was glad she could be honest about that. "Probably the opposite. You seem so completely professional. No one even talks about your love life anymore." As soon as she heard the words, Nina closed her eyes and lowered her head. "Maybe we should just shoot me now." She looked at him earnestly. "You may not believe me, but this is the least tactful I've been in my life. I'm usually too polite. My ex-husband called me Miss Manners."

"Not a compliment, I take it?"

"Not hardly."

Before David took a bite of his sandwich, he asked, "How long were you with your ex-husband?"

"We met when I was seventeen." She picked up her fork and began dissecting the scoop of tuna. "By nineteen I was pregnant with Isaac and by twenty-two I was having Izzy…alone."

"I remember."

Nina felt David's eyes on her as she toyed with her salad. "You do?"

He waited until she looked at him again. "I remember seeing you run out of Edward Karlson's retirement party when the garlic chicken was served. And I remember stepping off the elevator one day and watching you beeline toward the bathroom with your hand over your mouth."

"Oh, charming."

"You appeared to be pretty far along in your pregnancy by then. When I asked my secretary what was wrong, she said you were one of the unlucky women who had morning sickness for all nine months."

"True." The mere memory made Nina's tuna salad seem menacing, like a live shark. She looked ruefully at David. "It was miserable. Whatever I ate seemed to hit my stomach and bounce."

He winced. "And yet you were pregnant twice."

"Unintentionally the first time. But absolutely worth it."

"My secretary also said your marriage was failing. I checked the employee records. You didn't miss a day of work."

"You checked?"

David adjusted the knot of his tie. "Strictly business, Miss Baxter. You looked young enough to leave work and head straight for cheerleader practice. I wondered how you would handle two children, work and single parenthood. And then I realized you wore a sense of responsibility like some women wear expensive perfume—it followed you everywhere. I was impressed."

Dumbfounded, Nina fiddled with the paper napkin on her lap. "I'm not sure what to say. Is that why you sent the bear for Izzy? And the check?" Along with the gift of the bear, there had been a check for one hundred dollars. Perhaps naively, Nina had assumed that all pregnant employees received a cash gift. "Was that from the office…or from you?"

David began eating. After he swallowed the first bite of his sandwich, he said, "Does your ex-husband help with the kids? Time-wise? Financially?"

Nina decided that she knew enough about David Hanson now to know that if he chose not to respond to her question then the answer was yes. She was too discomfited by the discovery to push the topic. Keeping her eyes on her plate, she wondered why he'd taken special interest in her situation. Pity? Self-esteem had been hard to come by for a young woman whose husband had walked out. To know people had pitied her would have been too much to bear.

Though David had evaded her question, he was awaiting an answer to his. Nina toyed with her salad while she considered whether she wanted to talk about her ex and decided, *What the heck?*

"We never see him. The kids don't remember him. Parenthood didn't agree with Peter, and I didn't want to fight him for money." She shook her head. "In the end I suppose I thought it would be easier on the kids and me if he was out of our lives entirely. He didn't want to be a father or husband."

A muscle tightened in David's jaw. He stared at his plate, but his thoughts were clearly on something other than food.

Nina wondered if to his ears she sounded like a man-hater. That was far from the truth, but David Hanson had never married or had kids…that is, she didn't *think* he'd ever had kids. He kept his private life so private—who knew? Perhaps he could relate to the type of man her ex had turned out to be.

On that happy thought, Nina plunged her fork into her salad and chewed lettuce until David pinned her with his pensive gaze.

"In light of what you've shared with me, Miss Baxter, it seems like a good time to discuss the second half of my proposition."

Chapter Four

Friday afternoon had always been busy at Hanson Media Group. The end-of-the-week push, the force of George Hanson's larger-than-life personality and the sheer number of employees had often generated a sense of chaos.

Standing inside the door to his private office, David surveyed today's scene and thought his brother would rise from the grave if he could feel the tense and exhausted energy of the decimated Hanson staff. People did not bustle; they trudged through the tasks at hand, tasks that had multiplied since the last round of layoffs. It appeared to David that his employees felt overburdened and defeated before they even arrived at work.

They needed a pep talk; the kind George, who could have talked a snail into speeding, would have been able to give them.

The kind of pep talk David did not have inside him right now.

George had been twenty years David's senior, born when their parents were young, had the time and, presumably, the interest in a child—three conditions not present in David's youth. George had fit into the family better than David ever had. Like their father, he had been bigger than life and, as an adult, fascinated by money—making it, keeping it, flaunting it.

Even family dinners had revolved around business discussions, with George and George Sr. animatedly debating whether to merge or acquire. David recalled one evening in particular, when he was six or seven. He'd watched a superior episode of *Johnny Quest* on TV that day and believed that finally he had something worthwhile to share. His father had responded to his overeager, babbling recount by telling his mother they needed to fire the nanny; clearly she allowed him to watch inferior programming.

George hadn't said anything, just sipped his wine and grinned at his brother. From that time on, David had learned to please by being seen and not heard. At age ten he'd taken to wearing ties to school and listening intently at dinner so he could ask pertinent questions, whether the topic interested him or not.

David had not enjoyed hearing Nina's estimation of him yesterday, but she hadn't been off the mark. He'd been a stuffy, formal kid; it stood to reason he'd become a stuffy, formal man.

Lunch with Miss Baxter had happened four days ago; he'd been replaying it in his mind ever since. And accomplishing crap, because he couldn't get her…or the feeling of being with her…out of his mind.

Forcing himself away from the door, he headed down the hallway to his nephew Jack's office. Jack had temporarily taken George's place as CEO after his father's death. Perhaps he could rev up a skeleton staff that had stopped trusting the upper brass and had stopped thinking of Hanson as their company, too.

I know how they feel, David thought, scanning the empty desks as he passed down the hall. There were days—and today was one of them—when he thought he might be happier if he simply got out of the business and attempted something new.

He tried not to grit his teeth in an obvious way as he nodded to the employees who bothered to look up. He'd been dissatisfied for a long time; being with Nina Baxter highlighted his restlessness.

He'd had no word from her since their lunch. And that, he'd decided, was a direct result of the second half of his proposition.

When he reached Jack's door, he turned to Mrs. Wycliff, his nephew's secretary, who'd been with the company almost as long as David had himself. "Is he in?"

"He just buzzed me and asked that I hold all calls. I'll tell him you're here."

Before her fingers touched the phone, Jack's door jerked open. Barreling through, Jack, who was not normally a barreler, almost slammed into his uncle. "I'm on my way to see you." He blinked as if he were a bit disoriented by a circumstance he hadn't arranged.

"Here I am," David said helpfully.

Jack headed back into his office, then turned and told the woman whose hair had been gray as long as David could remember, "Hold all my calls."

"I got that part," David heard her murmur as he followed his nephew into the spacious corner office.

Jack hadn't changed the furnishings since his father had occupied this office, though his fiancée, Samantha, had clearly influenced the decor. Where a Waterford crystal bowl used to sit, there was now a large African basket filled with fresh fruit, and vibrant Mayan weavings had replaced the black-and-white Hirschfeld portrait George had commissioned of himself.

David saw the details in a way he hadn't before. The change in decor was more than superficial; it reflected the profound influence Samantha had on Jack's very personality. Of all George's children, his eldest son had been the least like his father. A conservative person at heart, Jack tended to keep the tones of his life low and mellow…at least he had before Samantha had upped the tempo.

"What kind of tie is that?" David peered at his nephew's neck.

"It's from Guatemala. It's woven." Jack patted the tie protectively, as if afraid his uncle might have something negative to say.

David shrugged. He wasn't going to slight his nephew's fashion statement. The material changes Samantha's presence had effected were nothing compared to the influence she had on Jack's personality. In fact, the recently relaxed and buoyant Jack hadn't looked this tense in awhile.

"What were you on your way to talk to me about?" David saw clearly that his nephew's thoughts were now on the woman who had undoubtedly purchased the tie, and he rather reluctantly brought Jack back to the business at hand. "You look like you need a long vacation. What tragedy has befallen Hanson Media today?"

David spoke tongue in cheek, but his concern spiked when the question etched deep furrows on his nephew's otherwise smooth face.

Jack remembered the letter in his hand and passed it toward his uncle. "Read this."

It took David mere seconds to realize that Hanson had, indeed, suffered another blow. He swore.

"I used that word in front of you when I was ten," Jack said, "and you threatened to wash my mouth out with the garden hose."

"I'm a lot older than you were." *And a lot more*

tired. David wanted to crumple the letter, toss it in the wastebasket, not give a damn. He was so freaking fed up with the chain reaction of problems his brother's deceit had left behind.

"Has anyone contacted Angel's Harbor yet?"

Jack shook his head. "I just got the letter."

Angel's Harbor was a group home for kids who had to be removed from their birth families, but for whom there was no foster care. Instead of further stressing an already overburdened foster-care system, Angel's Harbor was a not-for-profit alternative that sought to provide a safe and loving environment for kids in crisis. It was a great project, and Hanson Media was proudly one of the Harbor's biggest supporters. A large and celebrity-studded fund-raiser was coming up to generate the funds for a second Angel's Harbor in Illinois. Hanson Media was going to host the affair.

Or rather, had planned to host the affair. According to the legally worded letter in David's hand, Hanson's involvement through the years, "while greatly appreciated" was no longer "advisable." Apparently rumors of bankruptcy, layoffs and the recent problem of misrouting young Web visitors to a porn site made Hanson Media an undesirable name to have on one's sponsor list.

"This will be all over the media in twenty-four hours." David rubbed his eyes, but it would take more than a brief massage to stay the headache he felt building.

"What can we do?" Jack had never wanted to be the CEO of Hanson, but apparently he'd inherited enough of his father's competitive streak not to let the company die under his leadership.

"We try to make this better, and if we can't, we go shopping for another high-profile charity." Jack winced. "That sounds worse than it is," David assured. "Hanson has never supported an organization we didn't believe in. We're going to have to do some serious media schmoozing. You up for it?"

"Whatever it takes. Samantha will be onboard, too."

David nodded. He folded the letter, knowing he needed to get back to his office and start making phone calls. He felt overwhelmingly weary, though, a far cry from his usual response to business challenges.

Wandering to the wall of windows in Jack's office, he gazed at downtown Chicago. "Nice view," he murmured to Jack, then without any segue at all, asked, "How are things between you and Samantha?"

Turning to watch his nephew's reaction, David found himself fascinated by the transformation of Jack's features. Apparently the mere thought of the woman he loved was enough to wipe the concern from Jack's face. David didn't even need to hear the response, which was a simple "Great."

The sweeping restlessness that had plagued David lately hit again full force. Immediately he thought of Nina Baxter and her family, and of the feeling he'd had in their home…or, rather, he thought of the feeling in their home. The life, the exuberance, the familiarity among them.

He knew why he'd pushed so hard for Nina and her children to move in with him: He was like a leech, trying to feed off their happiness.

He had a disconnected family, and though he'd been physically intimate with women, he didn't feel that close to anyone.

"Do you want to come to dinner tonight?" Jack asked, clearly entertaining the idea on the spur of the moment. "Samantha's trying her hand at lasagna."

"Is she a good cook?"

"No. This recipe feeds ten. She's afraid she might ruin it if she cuts it down, so there'll be plenty."

David tried to remember the last time he'd had a non-business dinner with one of his nephews. Clinton had been in office.

Being an uncle to George's three boys had never come naturally. It might have gone better if the position had come with a job description. Or if David had figured out first what it meant to be a brother. As it was, despite being only nine years older than Jack, the oldest of his nephews, he'd always felt a bit awkward. A little too...formal.

Thank you, Nina, he thought wryly, *for giving voice to my conscience.*

He would definitely have dinner with Jack and Samantha. But not tonight. Tonight he would be awful company, and Jack didn't need an uncle who was moody and distracted. This time, he wanted to get the uncle business right.

"I think I'll let you do the first lasagna taste test," he said. "I'll take a rain check, though. Soon."

"All right. Deal." Jack gestured to the letter in David's hand. "Anything I can do to follow up on that?"

"I'll take care of it for now, but when the serious schmoozing starts, I'll let you know."

Jack nodded, but he was staring at the phone and fiddling with some wooden beads in a bowl on his desk, his mind obviously elsewhere.

"The reading of my father's will is coming up."

My father's, David thought, not *Dad's.* Jack's worried frown elicited a similar expression from his uncle. *If I had kids, I'd want them to call me Dad, even after I'm gone. And I wouldn't want them to look tense or nervous when they spoke about me.*

"What's on your mind, Jack?"

Exhaling forcefully, Jack said, "Evan and Andrew." He picked up a handful of the wooden beads then chucked them angrily back into the bowl. "My brothers haven't responded to Father's lawyer or to me. They were too busy to take an interest in the business. Now they're too 'busy' to be bothered with the will." Jack muttered an expletive.

Concern for his eldest nephew sparked David's irritation at Evan and Andrew. The younger Hanson brothers seemed to be MIA from the time they were old enough to say, "See you later." If they harbored resentment toward George, who had been a better boss than a father, that was one thing. But they were allowing Jack to shoulder the entire family burden, to upset his own life path in order to save a business that would ultimately benefit them, too. That was a circumstance David found intolerable.

Perhaps it was time to exercise an older relative's authority. Assuming this older relative had any.

"Have Mrs. Wycliff give me their contact information," he said to Jack, his tone sharp enough to indicate that he would not take no as an answer when he summoned his nephews home. "They'll be present for the reading of the will."

Jack nodded, obviously relieved to share one more burden he'd taken on after his father's sudden passing. "You don't mind dealing with this and the check?" He indicated the temporarily forgotten letter in David's hand.

"I don't mind," David assured. He felt fatigued by the problems his family continued to have, yet he realized that helping Jack made him feel more like an uncle, especially when he saw his nephew's shoulders relax. "You should take the rest of the day off," he said, surprising Jack and himself, too. "Help your fiancée make lasagna."

Jack's lips betrayed vestiges of the love-sodden smile he acquired now whenever Samantha was mentioned.

Exiting the office, David tried to focus on business

and not on his rapidly plunging mood. Ordinarily the letter he held would burn itself into his hand and his brain; his mind would wrap around that challenge and little else.

He told his secretary to hold all calls as he entered his office, but when he picked up his phone, it was not the charity's number he dialed.

Nina sat curled on one end of her couch, a magazine borrowed from the library in her lap. The article she'd been reading—"Six Home Businesses that Made a Million"—had turned out to be of little use. Unless she intended to conduct corporate headhunts out of her kitchen or mass-produce DVDs about achieving multiple orgasms, it was back to the drawing board job-wise. She glanced again at the article about multiple orgasms. Definitely not her area of expertise.

Closing the magazine self-consciously, she looked at her kids, who were home this Friday for a school in-service day. They sat in the living room with her, finishing their homework so they'd have the weekend free. Izzy used the family computer to write a book report and Zach was immersed in math. They each had a mug of hot apple cider and a toasted bagel sandwich next to them. As usual, Zach had eaten only the filling of his sandwich. It was a cozy scene. Nina sighed. She was such a good mother.

Except that she wasn't sure where they'd all be living next month and still hadn't mentioned her job loss to her children. She supposed she was still holding out hope for this Sunday's classifieds.

"Mom, how do you spell *porcupine?*" Izzy asked without looking up.

Zach jumped to the answer first. "P-o-r-c-u-p-i-n-e. Porcupine."

"Thanks, *Mom*."

Nina smiled, but weakly. Her children liked to study, God bless them. They deserved to go to college. They deserved music lessons and dance lessons and a class trip to New York to see *The Lion King* on-stage.

After her own parents had died and she'd moved in with Bubby, there had been little money for extras. To save Bubby from worrying about her, Nina had pretended not to want to go on "juvenile" school trips or to continue her "boring" violin lessons. She had watched her friends continue to be kids while she had grown up overnight. She didn't want her own children to face such concerns.

But how could she afford the extras when she was worried about keeping a roof over their heads?

Was it horrible of her not to leap at the opportunity David Hanson offered?

"Zach, do you want any more of that bagel?" she asked. In the past few days she'd gone from a nervous inability to eat to a nervous desire to eat everything in sight.

"Nope," her son answered.

"Toss it here." Part of her was so attracted to the idea of living in someone else's home with someone else's too-high rent and someone else's leaky faucets. She liked the idea of not worrying about the details for a while.

But she liked the idea of general peace of mind better, and she would not gain serenity by becoming dependent on the *idea* of David Hanson. And that's what would happen.

Because she'd been fantasizing about him all week already.

Burrowing more snugly into the corner of the couch, as if she thought she could hide there, she bit down hard on the chewy bagel. David Hanson was sophisticated, awkward, social, reserved, formal, funny—a study in contradictions. He was also solicitous, yet when he'd dropped the bomb about her moving into his apartment, he'd seemed forceful and protective.

And she'd liked that.

Shifting again and shoving the magazine with its money-making "multiples" idea between the sofa cushions, she thanked her lucky stars that Bubby was in a keno tournament at the senior center this week. Had she been able to hover over her granddaughter, the astute septuagenarian would have picked up immediately on Nina's restlessness and ambivalence.

David had stated that Nina's living situation was a

concern because he needed her on call in the evenings to oversee business parties, and he knew she would be more comfortable if her children were close by. Also, he didn't want her to be distracted by housing issues, which would certainly come up again. Even if she hadn't been laid off, she'd have struggled with the rent increase, and she couldn't imagine finding lower rent in a decent neighbourhood.

Nina didn't know if David was a control freak or boss of the year. She didn't know whether to accept his offer and deal with the disturbing thoughts she'd been having about him or to reject the job outright and put the Hansons—David especially—out of her mind. Socially, he was way out of her league. Romantically, they weren't even on the same planet. She'd married at eighteen. He was still single at forty-four.

Why was he still single at forty-four? Nina frowned, working her jaws around another big bite of the bagel. Was it a chronic condition? Lord knew he hadn't suffered for a lack of exquisite female companionship over the years. He'd been photographed with some of the loveliest women in Chicago.

Photographed with them. But never married. Nina couldn't recall even a rumor about an engagement. Did David Hanson date for publicity? Could he be—

Nina looked at her children, making sure they were focused on their work, as if they'd be able to read her thoughts if they looked at her.

Gorgeous, formal, a little awkward, never married...

What if David Hanson was gay and trying to hide it?

She began to chew the bagel with nervous intensity. The more she thought about it, the more it made a kind of sense. Hanson Media garnered much of its financial support from family-slanted groups. The kind that typically frowned on alternative lifestyles. And certainly, after the problems with his brother and the Internet gaffe, now would not be the time to come out of the closet.

If David Hanson turned out to be gay, Nina wouldn't have to brood a bit about her silly attraction. Or that odd feeling of wanting to be taken care of. All that would be a moot point.

In that case, she could kind of, almost, sort of see herself accepting the job offer.

"I'll get it!" Izzy jumped up.

"Get what?" Nina said around a cheekful of bagel before she realized the phone was ringing.

Call it a sixth sense, which she'd never really possessed, but somehow she knew who was on the phone before her daughter returned, holding out the receiver.

"He asked to speak with 'Miss Baxter,'" Izzy said in a stage whisper that left much to be desired, and grinning girlishly as if this were hysterically funny.

Nina didn't bother to ask *who?* "Well, I'm not

married anymore," she reminded her daughter as she unfurled from the sofa and stood on cramped legs. Shooing her nosy child back to the computer, she stumbled to the kitchen before her knees had warmed up and held the receiver to her ear. "Hello."

"What should I call you?"

David's voice was smooth and rich, as always. And, as always, she detected a little frown in his tone.

"Miss Baxter is fine," she said. She kept her married name because it belonged to her children, too, but asking people to call her Ms. was too much trouble. Most people called her "Mrs."; she didn't bother to correct them. "Or you can call me 'Nina,'" she added. "Your brother always called us by our first names."

"Yes." Nina heard him sigh as if the mention of his brother were a heavy weight. "He should have run the PR department."

"You seem to do all right."

"Apparently not," David countered. "I can't even get prospective employees to phone me."

She winced. "Guilty. Sorry. I've been…" she hesitated.

"Busy?" he supplied. "Searching the classifieds? Ambivalent?"

Tucking the phone between her shoulder and cheek, Nina smiled reluctantly as she opened the refrigerator and poked at a defrosting chicken. "All of the above," she admitted.

"Hmm. And did you find anything in the classifieds?"

Why lie? "No. Not yet."

"And you are still searching, because…?"

Leaving the poor chicken alone, she shut the refrigerator and walked to the window to put a little more distance between her and the living room. Quietly she said into the phone, "Because having an office job and my own apartment would be less complicated than working and living in someone else's home."

"Not if you can't find a job or an apartment to suit your situation," he said with a characteristic businessman's confidence. "My offer is actually less challenging than trying to find and maintain housing given Chicago rents and the fact that you need at least a two-bedroom place. And very few office jobs will allow the adequate time and flexibility to parent your children without significant child care. I'm sure you've already come to that conclusion, which must be why you haven't phoned to categorically reject my offer."

"Well, now that we've worked that out," Nina mumbled, gazing out the window at the old neighborhood in which they lived.

He was correct about thing: She and her children were going to have to move. She couldn't come up with the rent the new owners of the building had requested. She'd already asked for a break on the basis of being a good tenant of long-standing. It was a long shot, but she'd had to try. Unfortunately she'd received only a swift and politely worded response thanking her for her loyalty to the apartment complex and rejecting her request.

"I have more questions," she told David. "About the job. And the living situation."

"Name the time and place," he said, understanding before she said a word that she didn't want to discuss this over the phone.

"Your schedule is fuller than mine. At the moment."

"Tonight. Seven o'clock."

The one night she had restrictions. "It's Shabbat—the Jewish Sabbath," she said. "The kids and I are serving shabbos dinner at my grandmother's senior center. The other servers are down with the flu, so I can't cancel."

The pause on the other end of the phone was brief. "Need an extra pair of hands?"

The pause on Nina's end of the line was quite a bit longer. "You?"

"I'm free tonight." He sounded offhand, as if he volunteered to serve challah and Manischewitz wine to seniors whenever he had an open Friday. "Just give me a street address and a time."

"I don't think that will be the best place—"

"Serving usually requires some cleaning. That ought to give us a few minutes." She heard him shuffle papers. "I've got to go. Give me an address and a time, and I'll meet you there. You can ask your questions or watch me wash dishes while you come up with an alternative meeting."

"Wouldn't it be easier to just—"

"Address and time, Miss Baxter. I'm on the clock."

She came up with the requested information, and they hung up.

Nina gazed out the window and amended her opinion of David Hanson. He might be concerned and genuine, but he was also wily and persistent and surprisingly skilled at getting his way.

Once more, she wanted to kick herself in the tush for being charmed by his tactics.

She shook her head and tried to ignore the desire to race to her closet and try on clothes. She wasn't sure what else she was going to discover about David tonight or how it would affect her decision to take the job. But suddenly, that was not her greatest worry. She was far more concerned with all the things she was discovering about herself when David was around.

Chapter Five

Fifteen minutes into Shabbat, Nina decided David had to be gay, after all. No straight man she'd ever met was as willing to have his cheeks pinched by senior citizens as he was.

Bubby was overjoyed to see her "Davy." She introduced him to her friends as "My Nina's David. You know, used to be her boss. He likes to come visit."

Likes to come visit may have been an overstatement; they'd only seen him twice outside of work in thirteen years, but the comment had the desired effect on Bubby's friends. For years, the denizens of the Wilkens Senior Center had read about the Hansons, Chicago's upper crust. Bubby had made sure of that. She'd brought in every newspaper clipping that had anything to do with the Hansons since Nina had started working for the company in 1993. Now her women friends were meeting a Hanson in person, and they were positively giddy. Only bringing in Oprah would have been a better show-and-tell.

One of Bubby's octogenarian gal pals tried to coax David into sitting down to dinner, but he declined, reminding her that he was there to serve, not to be served. In all these years, it was the first time Nina had seen him turn on the charm, and she realized he had an abundance of it.

When the last bite of kugel was eaten and the plates cleared, Nina told her children to head to the multipurpose room to join the services.

"We're supposed to help the whole night," Izzy protested, though Isaac, who loved Friday services, was already halfway out the kitchen door.

"Mr. Hanson is here to help me," Nina said. "And I don't want you to miss Rabbi Jackie. She's a Renewal rabbi visiting from California. I'd like you to hear a woman rabbi."

Izzy, who had learned from her mother and grandmother that women had not even been allowed to hold the Torah when Bubby was a girl, appeared unconvinced.

"And, I understand she raises quarter horses," Nina added. "I'm sure she'll talk to you about that after the services."

Bingo.

Izzy raced her brother to the multipurpose room, leaving Nina alone with David in the kitchen.

Nina stood at the sink, which was filled with dirty dishes, and watched David sample a chocolate-chip *rugelach* from the dessert tray they would bring out later. `

"What are you doing?" she asked him.

He looked up from the cookie and smiled. "Sorry. I couldn't help myself." Popping the rest of the cookie into his mouth, he spoke around it. "Let's get to work."

He appeared so boyish, so ingenuous, Nina had a crazy impulse to hug him as he approached the sink and stopped in front of her. He was still wearing his dress shirt from work, but the sleeves were rolled up and his tie was loosened. So formal. She shook her head.

"That's not what I mean. I mean, what are you doing *here?* Why were you cutting kugel for two dozen octogenarians when I know you could have found twenty free minutes to meet with me?"

"What's *koo-gul?*"

"The noodle casserole."

"The one that smelled like cinnamon?"

"Yes."

"I wanted to try that." He glanced around.

"It's all gone. Don't change the subject." Grabbing a dish towel, she flicked him on the middle with it. But privately she added *cute* to the list of descriptive adjectives she was compiling about him. "You aren't here for the food," she insisted. "What's the deal? Is Hanson targeting seniors as a hot market? Are you building a Web zine for the over-eighty crowd?"

Golden-brown eyebrows lowered over almost similarly golden-brown eyes. David's lower lip jutted beyond its mate. The expression made Nina instantly sorry she had teased him, and she told him she was kidding. "I just can't figure out why you wanted to meet here, that's all."

"I suppose I thought you'd be more relaxed on familiar turf," he admitted. "More yourself. I want you to work for me, Nina. I didn't want to sit across a table from you while you come up with a hundred sound reasons to turn me down."

"You think there are a hundred sound reasons for me to turn you down?"

"I think there are a few," he said honestly, looking her straight in the eye. "But I think there are more reasons to say yes, and they're just as sound."

The hair he usually wore brushed straight back had gotten mussed during his runs from kitchen to table. A gold-tinged lock fell over his forehead. Nina put both hands behind her back and clutched the towel, resisting the urge to reach up and push his hair off his brow if only to see how he would respond.

"Why do you want to hire me? It's certainly more complicated than hiring someone who has no dependents. Not to mention secure housing."

David nodded slowly. For well over an hour now, he'd been with Nina, working under her direction, putting food on plates held out to him by quivering veined hands and watching her fill needs both practical and emotional. Nina's warmth and genuine interest in others spread over the people in her immediate vicinity like the perfect blanket on a chilly night. Watching her, feeling her beside him, he became more and more convinced that his *life* was a chilly night.

He began to wonder if he was heading toward a midlife crisis, dissatisfied suddenly with a path that had suited him well until now.

"I like your dependents," he said carefully, keeping his voice light and casual. He didn't want to scare her away. He didn't want to scare himself. He didn't know what he wanted from her, really. It seemed pathetic to believe that he wanted to borrow her life for a while, to experience family by sharing the one she had created with such obvious care. David feared that might be the truth, however, as his own parents' agenda had not included making their youngest child feel warm and fuzzy.

He looked at the lovely blonde who was watching him closely with a wariness and suspicion he probably merited. She'd dressed nicely but conservatively in a pale blue sweater and long wool skirt. Her hair was pulled back in a thick bun, but she hadn't completely tamed the curls. He liked that.

"Nina," he said, the first time tonight that he'd used her given name. Up to now he'd stuck with *Miss Baxter,* which had made the old women smile. "You have the qualities I want in a personal assistant." He decided to keep his reply and his thoughts on the business plane. "I can enumerate your assets if you like. You're efficient, a fast thinker, easy to get along with—" Her brows shot up, and David smiled. "I like people who tell me the truth. You're also warm and gracious, which will be critical at the business functions I'll expect you to supervise and attend. And, you're available. That's not good for you, but it does work out for me. I don't have time to interview people."

"Your secretary could—"

"She has more than enough to do right now."

"I have children. Have you ever lived with two pre-teenage children?"

He rested his palm on the sink, leaning into it. "No. I don't have kids of my own. I'm not planning to have kids of my own. But yours are already housebroken, and they seem docile enough."

He enjoyed the rich, free sound of her laughter. "Housebroken and docile, huh? You sure you don't want to hire someone with, say, a Boston terrier?" She shook her head. "You **cannot** count on my kids to be quiet."

"Silence is overrated."

"They're messy. I **don't want** to worry that we're

ruining a Persian rug every time Isaac brings mud in. And Izzy likes to tap dance on hard surfaces."

"I have wall-to-wall carpeting."

Nina began to chew her lip—unconsciously, he thought. "I need the job," she murmured, and though he heard the reluctance in her inflection, the hope that grew in his chest felt surprisingly good.

Angling toward the sink, she turned on the faucets to fill the basin.

David picked up a sponge. "I'll wash this time. You dry."

She eyed him doubtfully, but didn't demur. Instead, she pulled two aprons out of a drawer, insisted he don one and rolled up her sleeves to swish bubbles into the soapy water.

"Have at it, mister."

As they began to clean the dinner mess, the sound of voices raised in song drifted in from the multipurpose room. The melody was moving and joyful, but the Hebrew words were unfamiliar to David. He was about to ask what they meant when he heard Nina begin to sing softly under her breath.

Silently he handed her the wet plates he had scrubbed and stole glances at her profile. Somehow, from her lips the foreign words acquired meaning for him. He could tell that the song was filled with anticipation, that it was about waiting and hoping for something.

Nina Baxter, he decided, was beautiful. With curly

blond hair, baby-doll blue eyes and a figure like Betty Boop's, she could easily be termed *cute* or *adorable;* but that would discount the depth of her attractiveness. She was a woman, certainly not the girl who'd first come to work over a decade ago.

As she sang, her soft features seemed to mature before his eyes. The song held meaning for her. He had no intention of interrupting and was content to work and listen to her sing, but she stopped abruptly to ask, "Have you ever wanted children?"

Caught off guard, he didn't temper his response. "No."

She looked mildly surprised, but not disappointed. "That's it, huh? Just 'no'? Have you ever thought about it? Or is it something you've actively avoided?"

The pan David was scrubbing slipped from his fingers and clattered into the sink. Frowning, he fished it out, made sure no harm was done and wondered just how complete his answer ought to be. There were lines of decorum, he'd always felt, that shouldn't be crossed. Somehow, though, with Nina he wasn't at all certain the usual rules applied. "All right, I'm going to be blunt here. My answer involves you."

This time, Nina's head reared back with considerable surprise. David kept working, but angled his attention toward Nina. "I remember when you were pregnant for the second time and not throwing up in a business meeting seemed like a Herculean effort for you. Then I found out you were single and had to make a living on your own…." He narrowed his eyes in an expression both wry and a bit sheepish. "I went out," he admitted, "and bought a very large box of condoms."

Nina stopped drying a water glass. She blinked at him. "That was *really* honest."

"You asked."

"So what was the deal, exactly? You didn't trust the woman to use birth control? You didn't trust yourself to stick around if you did make a baby?"

He scowled and spontaneously flicked sudsy water at her nose, not something he recalled ever doing to a woman—or an employee—before. "No. Jeez, no. I trusted myself to act with integrity." He shook his head, working harder to scrape some kind of casserole out of a pan. "I didn't trust myself to act with joy—that was the problem. I thought a child— and a woman—deserved both."

After a pause, Nina responded softly, "You're right. On both counts." She kept her eyes on the glass she was still drying…well beyond the point of dryness…then looked up at him. "Hey, so you're not—"

She cut herself off.

"What?" David gazed at her. Her expression was five parts surprise, five parts mortification. "Don't stop now. We're building trust here. I'm not…?"

"Not…going…to get the stuff off the pan that

way. Use the scrubber." She nodded to a nylon ball on the sink.

He cocked a brow at her, tossed the sponge aside and picked up the scrubber. "I'm not what, Nina? Come on, cough it up. You were about to insult me again. It's all over your face."

Nina considered a fervent denial, but fervently *lying* on the Sabbath would·be bad karma. Also, David didn't seem particularly disturbed by the prospect of her insulting him again.

"It's not an insult this time. Really," she said, setting aside the glass she'd wiped to a squeaky-clean shine and turning her focus on a dinner plate. "I'd just wondered—just briefly, I mean I didn't dwell on it— whether you hadn't married because you might be…" She lowered her head, not at all sure she should say it. "…ay."

"What?" He leaned toward her. "I didn't catch the last word."

She mumbled it a second time.

"I can't understand you. I might be what?" He shook his head. "Gray?"

"No! Gay," she said loudly and clearly. "I thought maybe you were gay."

He looked utterly shocked. Speechless, in fact.

"It's a reasonable assumption," she defended.

"Really?"

She stood her ground and looked up at him. *Now* he seemed a little peeved.

Nina sighed and set the plate on top of some others. "You see? This is why a boss and a secretary should not even contemplate living together. We're going to cross all kinds of unspoken boundaries."

"No, I think this one *is* spoken."

"Well, I didn't mean anything negative."

"That settles it, you're moving in. My reputation is at stake."

"If you and I move in together—with my children—*your* reputation is the last thing we're going to worry about," she contradicted, the topic of his sexuality losing ground to the issue of her children's well-being. "I will insist that we make it very clear to everybody that there is nothing romantic or sexual going on. I won't even consider moving in unless we're agreed on that."

"Agreed that there *is* nothing romantic or sexual going on or agreed that we *tell* people there is nothing romantic or sexual going on?"

She folded her arms.

"All right. I will take swift and decisive action to correct any mistaken impressions. Including my own. Kidding," David said when she opened her mouth to retort. "Meet me at my place, Sunday. I'll show you around, you can ask invasive questions and make your decision."

Temporarily nonplussed, Nina stared.

"This is the easy part, Miss Baxter. Just say yes to Sunday. We'll take it from there."

* * *

Two days later, on a Sunday afternoon, David stood in the steamy bathroom of his downtown condo and slapped cologne on his freshly shaved face and neck.

Nina was due to arrive to inspect his place at 4:00 p.m. And he was preparing for their meeting as if he were about to embark on the hottest date of his life.

Setting the cologne on the granite counter, he abandoned his preparations and headed for the kitchen. This wasn't a date, but he did want her to say, "Yes." Yes, she would work for him; yes, she and her kids would move in. His reasons, he had decided while he'd run on the treadmill this morning and again as he'd pushed through several sets of flies, were sound. She'd be a great personal assistant, and if she worked for him he could stop feeling guilty that she'd been fired. He was thinking clearly.

When the doorbell rang, he was downing a glass of orange juice and blaming it for the sudden burn in his stomach.

His heart began to pound uncomfortably as he walked to the door. *Damned acidic fruit juices.*

Nina stood in the large light-filled hall of his twenty-third-floor condo and met his gaze with what he was coming to view as her characteristic this-will-never-ever-work expression.

Standing so close he could smell her shampoo, she said, "This will never ever work," before she bothered with "Hello."

David smiled, a deep smile that started low and rose until it parted his lips in a full-fledged grin. The sight of her relaxed him.

"Bummer, Miss Baxter." He put a hand beneath her elbow. "Come in."

Nina tugged on the lapel of her long coat. It was lightweight for spring, a powder-blue color that looked great with her eyes. "All right," she agreed. "But only because I've never seen an apartment like this before, and I'm curious. *Not* because I'm still considering moving in, because now that I've seen this building—" She silenced abruptly as they entered the living room. "You said you had carpeting."

David looked at the room, genuinely bemused. "Ahh, yes, I do."

"It's white," Nina said in a tone that sounded faintly accusing. All David could think about was taking her coat off so he could see how she was dressed today. So far he'd liked her best in the jeans she'd worn the day she'd lobbed office supplies at him.

"Sort of off-white-cream-ish, don't you think?" he suggested, hoping that whatever perturbed her about white carpeting would not stand in the way of their sitting down to the chardonnay and cheese tray he'd picked up at the wine shop near his gym.

"Actually, I'd call this particular hue Do-You-Have-Any-Idea-What-Grape-Juice-Does-to-a-Deep-Pile white."

"Oh." He smiled. "No, I don't. You'll have to explain it to me. In great detail. May I take your coat?"

After a moment, Nina shrugged out of the thin wrap. "Okay, but only because it's warm in here, and I have a feeling the tour will take a while, because this place is mammoth."

David inclined his head agreeably. She sounded less than approving again, but she was here, and she was staying. He was getting what he wanted. Who was he to argue?

About to say he'd hang the coat up, he decided to toss it over the leather sofa instead. Obviously Nina was having a problem with the formality of his apartment relative to the casualness of her lifestyle. So he'd show her what a casual guy he really was.

Following the direction her coat took, she smoothed a hand over the arm of the sectional couch and whistled in appreciation. "Is this Corinthian leather?"

He nodded in satisfaction. All right, at last she'd found something to admire. The fact that he had no idea what kind of leather adorned his sofa did not stop him from answering, "Yes, it is."

"Uh-huh." She clucked her tongue. "One good jab from a ballpoint pen, and that's a goner."

She was beginning to sound like an inspector for *Better Homes and Gardens* child-proofing edition. David put a hand on the small of her back.

"Come on. Let's get out of here before you notice

the Chihuly glass bowl waiting to be shattered by one good tap of a Nerf ball."

"My kids don't have Nerf balls," she said, allowing him to guide her toward the kitchen. "They have the hard rubber, dangerous kind. I'm only thinking of you."

"Miss Baxter," David murmured as he nudged her ahead of him and sneaked a look at her jean-clad tush, "you've no idea how those words comfort me. Please believe me when I say I'm thinking of you, too."

Chapter Six

Nina knew she was being disagreeable. She even knew why.

Knowing for sure that David wasn't gay had allowed all sorts of annoying fantasies to disturb her sleep the past two nights.

There was no denying it: She found him attractive, in a what-are-you-out-of-your-mind-he's-your-boss-and-completely-inappropriate-for-you kind of way. Moving in with him would be a disaster—capital *D*, capital *Isaster*.

Which was why she was smart to point out all the flaws in his reasoning.

"Oh wow, you have a stainless-steel fridge." She

ran her hand admiringly along the handle. "Aren't these great? I mean, if you don't have kids. Once you have kids, of course, stainless is the last finish you want on an appliance. They never look clean." She tapped the refrigerator door with her fingernail. "All fingerprints, all the time."

"I'll remember that, Heloise."

"I'm just—"

"Thinking of me." David nodded. "You've got my back."

He took two steps toward her, pressed his palm flat against the freezer door—which would leave a terrible mark—and loomed over her. "I have a nice chardonnay chilling in this impractical refrigerator. Would you like a glass? It might help you relax."

"I don't need to relax."

"Oh, yeah." He nodded broadly. "You do."

"Well!"

Nina tried to glance away. David wasn't encroaching on her space, exactly. He hardly ever did that, she'd noticed. He was far too upright—figuratively and literally. He stood as straight as a tree most of the time. When he leaned toward her, he did it with his eyes.

"I picked up some cheese, too," he said.

Nina's gaze snapped back to him. He didn't look particularly flirtatious. "You bought wine and cheese? For a quick business meeting?"

David angled his head and frowned. "Too stuffy?"

He moved to a cabinet, opened it and looked in. "How about cherry cola and a peanut-butter Ritz?" When she didn't answer, he poked around some more. "Corn curls and apple juice? Molasses snaps? Scooter Pie? Aw, there's only one left." He angled his gaze toward her. "It's vanilla, not my favorite. I suppose I could let you have it."

"Scooter Pies?" she said, incapable of not smiling. "*You* eat all this stuff?"

"Yes, I'm really a casual person, Miss Baxter. Very informal. Just a big kid myself. I get fingerprints all over the refrigerator, too. Cheese-puff crumbs on the bedspread." He wagged his head. "Johanna gets very annoyed with me."

Nina felt the smile slip from her face. "Who's Johanna?"

"My housekeeper. She comes once a week. I was going to hire her another day if you and your kids moved in, which would help her out, but if it's just me there's not enough for her to do." He tossed the information off casually, as if it weren't a tactic to make her agree to the job and the accommodations. "All right, let's see…. I also have chililime tortilla chips." His eyes darted her way. "I won't mention the garlic if you don't mention the garlic."

"I thought you said you rarely eat at home."

His grin was infectious. "You call this eating?" He rooted through the cabinet some more. "Bag of chocolate chips…cinnamon graham crackers…beer nuts… stop me if I'm getting warmer."

Nina swallowed the lump in her throat. *He* wasn't getting warmer, but *she* was. Darn him, why did he have to be…cute? He stretched up to reach the top shelf of the cabinet, and his polo shirt lifted above the waistband of his jeans to reveal a lean, flat middle. When Nina leaned her head a little to the right, she was pretty sure she glimpsed a hint of washboard abs. He was handsome in his suits, yes, but she'd never guessed that he kept himself so fit.

"Do you bring women here?" she blurted with no preamble, save for the one in her own head. "I mean, often? Do you bring them home often…on dates? I'm only asking because I have impressionable preteens, and if I were to consider your offer—which I'm really not—but in case I were suddenly to consider it, I would need to know."

He turned toward her. "If you and your children were to move in—which you are not—but *if* you were suddenly to consider it, you have my word that I would not bring women home."

And that should have been that.

But David's response referred to the future, and Nina was asking about the past and the present, too. Which was obviously none of her business and which had nothing to do with her children's welfare. Darn it.

Leaving her post by the refrigerator, she pointed

to a beautiful carved wood door with an etched-glass insert. "What's through here?"

David came up behind her, reached above her head to place a hand on the door and pushed. "Dining area. For casual evenings at home."

The irony of his words struck full-force with Nina's first glimpse of the room. *Formal dining room* would be a criminal understatement to describe the space she walked into.

"Wow."

Huge and decorated to the hilt, the room held a table that seated ten without inserts, a majestic chandelier, and walls covered in a quilted champagne-colored silk.

Nina ran her hands over the back of a chair that had pale striped-silk upholstery and carved blond wood. "Is this where the president sits?"

David joined her next to the chair and sighed. "You're about to tell me what ketchup would do to these chairs, aren't you?"

"Not at all. Because I highly doubt that anything served at this table would require ketchup."

She turned to face him. Deliberately, she had worn her customary Sunday-with-the-kids attire: jeans that were faded because she'd worn them for years not because she was making a fashion statement, a cropped lilac sweater, a pair of clogs. Her hair was scraped into a ponytail, so it looked neat until it reached a thick elastic band and burst into the usual ringlets.

As relatively casual as David appeared today—and he was definitely dressed more casually than she had ever seen him—he still gave the appearance of being neat and conservative. And rich. His leather shoes looked as expensive as his couch.

"I'm not used to all this luxury, that's all," she answered him. "Forgive me if I gawk, but this is like one of those holiday home tours, minus the eggnog."

"I knew I forgot something." He snapped his fingers then laid his hand on the back of the chair, close enough to her hand to make her fidget. "I'll show you the rest of the house."

He led her through the apartment with ease and an enviable nonchalance. Obviously David wasn't overly impressed with his own possessions, but neither did he ignore the impact they had on her, particularly when he and Nina entered the library. Nina heard herself sigh.

The room was a reader's dream. Wall-to-wall carved wood bookshelves, ambient lighting, reading nooks with the kind of chairs you could disappear in. There were books of all kinds. Her children, especially Zach, who loved to read and seemed to have no preference regarding subject matter, would go nuts.

"You even have children's books," Nina said, running her fingers along the spines of hardcover editions of *Harry Potter* and *Lemony Snicket*.

"We have a children's Web site. Gotta keep up." David stood behind her, casually shrugging off the answer.

Nina walked her fingers down the row of books. "You have *A Wrinkle in Time...Roll of Thunder, Hear My Cry...Where the Red Fern Grows....* I bet most of the kids who visit the Web site have never heard of these books."

"Yes they have. I post there."

Surprised and interested to know more, she turned, but David was already walking to the door. He spent time on the Hanson kids' Web site? He posted? Talked to kids? Suggested books? He truly was full of surprises. And his library was designed for use, not merely for looks. What would the other books say about their owner?

Apparently he wasn't going to give her time to find out. David was already heading down the hall by the time she exited the library. She had to trot to catch up. Standing once more in the living room, she realized they'd made a wide U.

"And that completes our tour. Sorry about the eggnog. Check back with us at the holidays." He offered the smile she was coming to think of as gentle and a bit goofy.

In truth, though aspects of his apartment were decidedly elegant and far grander than what she was used to, nothing here was tasteless or overdone, and the rooms that were truly David's—like the library—were perfect.

"So, what's the verdict?" he asked, smile still in place, tone casual.

After a few sarcastic cracks about the formality of the rooms, Nina welcomed the chance to make amends. "It's a wonderful apartment. Really. Sophisticated, but warm. And I'm sure the dining room is exactly what your guests expect—"

"I'm not asking for a critique of the decor." David waved a hand. "Move in and redecorate for all I care. I'm asking whether you're taking the job." He paused, holding eye contact. "I need an assistant soon. You've seen the apartment." He spread his arms. "You've seen me. What's your decision?"

Outstanding bills, the threat of homelessness, fear of failure nipped at Nina's heels, urging her to jump at the job, but she remained as disturbed by the solution as she was by the problem. If she said yes and fell in with his plan, what next? Move in lock, stock and barrel? How would she keep her distance from the boss whose eyes and decency drew her like magnets?

When several bars of upbeat music interrupted the moment, she felt a whoosh of relief. "My cell phone!"

David arched a brow.

"It could be important," she apologized, trying not to exhibit excessive gratitude for the time out as she ran toward her purse. Generally when her cell phone trilled on a weekend, the caller was her grandmother, asking the name of George Clooney's pet pig so she could win a bet with someone at the senior center.

Flipping open the phone, Nina endeavored to answer with more professionalism than her usual, "Hey, Bubby."

For several long moments, all she did was listen. Then she nodded, croaked, "I'll be right there," and snapped the phone shut.

Scooping her purse over her arm and grabbing up her coat, she headed immediately for the door. "I have to go," she muttered, turning at the last minute toward David, who looked as if he'd expected this.

"I really have to go," she said, struggling to stay calm while her chest constricted. "Isaac is in the hospital."

David insisted on driving Nina to the emergency room, and he kept a steadying hand beneath her arm as they walked in, unsure exactly of Isaac's status. The boy had been playing ball at a friend's house when he'd collapsed with an asthma attack. David was not sure who looked more ashen when they were finally by Isaac's bedside—the boy or his mother. Nina enveloped her son in a tight maternal hold, and the preteen didn't seem to mind at all.

"I couldn't get my breath this time," he whispered in his mother's ear while she stroked the back of his head.

Nina's own terror—she'd been silent the entire car ride—was put aside so she could be strong for her son. "I know, baby. I'm here now. You'll be fine. Everything will be fine."

Simple words, but Nina's attendance allowed Isaac to relax. There was magic in her love, in the trust she'd inspired in her children. It soothed. It convinced.

David hung back, but no one questioned his presence, so he stayed to hear the E.R. doctor's opinion that Zach should carry a stronger inhaler from now on. He cautioned against overexertion, an admonition Zach had heard too many times before. David could see Nina's frustration, and he decided to take the steps he'd have taken for his own child. He slipped from the room and made a call.

When Zach and Nina emerged from the E.R., he handed her a piece of paper with a phone number plus the date and time of Zach's appointment with the head of cardiopulmonary at the hospital.

Nina frowned at the paper then turned to her son. "Here's some change for the vending machine, Zachie. You must be starving. Get something decent, like trail mix."

"How about a Baby Ruth? That has peanuts."

"How about trail mix?" she reiterated, and Zach ran off. Nina raised the paper David had given her. "I don't understand. This is a specialist. We weren't referred to a specialist. Where'd you get this?"

"Phil Reed is a friend of mine," David said, trying to keep pride out of his voice, because in truth he felt damned good about being able to help. "We went to school together. Call his office first thing tomorrow, and they'll set up an appointment."

"It's Sunday. Did you call him at home?"

David smiled. "He owes me a favor or two. He didn't mind."

Nina held the paper up as if it were a note from her kids' principal, the kind of thing she didn't want to see. Keeping her voice low, so Zach wouldn't overhear, she said, "We can't see a specialist, because we weren't referred. My insurance won't cover it. Not to mention, I'm not sure how much longer I will even have insurance. There's no way I can afford to take Zach to the head of a pulmonary department. Those guys charge a fortune for saying, *How are you today?*"

Tears David didn't understand sparkled in Nina's blue eyes. He thought she was angry with him until he realized that her anger was directed inward. Shame and frustration tightened her lips and the fist that clutched the now-crumpled note.

"So Zach hasn't seen a specialist in a while?" he ventured, despite her obvious resistance to the conversation. "He doesn't visit one on a regular basis?"

"What planet are you from? The one where there really was health-care reform?"

David scowled. "All right, I get the picture. But fortunately I know Phil…" He stopped himself. Nina's face revealed every emotion: hope, worry, anticipation and ultimately the absolute unwillingness to let him foot the bill. She shook her head.

David felt as frustrated as she looked. "Zach needs this."

"I know!"

"What do you suggest?"

Together they looked toward Zach, who was still trying to decide which button to push on the vending machine.

Nina divided her gaze between her son and David and finally asked, "Does the job come with health benefits?"

"Yes."

"I'll take it."

It was a sunny, windy Saturday morning when Nina and her children moved out of their apartment. Zach had an appointment with Dr. Reed the following Monday morning, and Nina wanted to be settled in their new accomodations by then.

Goodwill had already picked up the larger pieces of furniture Nina didn't need, as David's place was already furnished. Because she drove a compact car, she had rented a small van to haul their TV and the boxes that held all their worldly goods. There wasn't much to shout about.

The kids were indoors, finishing their packing, while Nina lugged boxes to the van. Fearing hernias and unwilling to listen to Bubby complain about having to wear a truss the rest of her life, Nina had banished her grandmother from the proceedings.

Likewise, she'd insisted that Zach fill boxes rather than carry them; she did not want to risk triggering another asthma attack. So, despite the wind and the fact that it was only 11:00 a.m., perspiration made Nina feel soggy and sticky beneath her T-shirt.

Grunting, she hefted the TV onto the van then tried to wriggle it farther into the cargo area. Sweat trickled from beneath her baseball cap.

"I figured."

The displeased tone came from directly behind her. Nina whirled, lost her balance and landed on an elbow on the van floor.

"What are you doing here, and what do you mean, you 'figured'?" Nina demanded as she struggled up. She wiped sweat from her eyes and silently cursed David Hanson for looking like an ad for Lands' End while she resembled a street kid.

Taking her gently but firmly by the shoulders, David pulled her away from the van, climbed aboard and carried the TV all the way to the back. Then, without speaking, he rearranged boxes until they were stacked precisely, so that they fit together like a puzzle, keeping each other in place. When he was satisfied, he jumped down and confronted her on the sidewalk.

"I figured you'd be out here, attempting to move everything by yourself. You are one of the most stubborn women I've ever met." He out-scowled her and demanded, "Where are the high-school boys you said you were going to hire?"

"They wanted eighteen dollars an hour, plus breaks every two hours. You'd think they were unionized. I don't have that much stuff, I can do it myself." She planted both fists on her hips and said, "You told me you'd be working all day." Despite the fact that she and her kids were moving into his condo, Nina had wanted to ease into the new environment without his presence for the first couple of hours.

"You agreed to call if you needed help."

"You agreed to keep quiet and let me do this my way."

"You said your way would be fast and simple."

Nina narrowed her gaze. "Evidently neither one of us can be trusted."

"Evidently." David smiled broadly. "Miss Baxter, I predict that we will make an excellent team. Stay here and guard the TV," he directed. "I'll get the rest of your things."

"No way. This is my show. I'm running it. *You* stay here. I'll get the rest of our stuff."

"You want me to stand here, watching a van while you carry boxes down two flights of stairs?" He crossed his arms high on his chest, rocked back on his heels and slowly shook his head. "Nothing doing. Less than a week ago you suggested I might be gay. My masculinity won't survive another hit."

Observing the belligerent posture, Nina could barely suppress a grin. "You look like Mr. Clean." He refused to budge. "All right." Sighing, she dug into her jeans pocket and pulled out a quarter. "We'll flip to see who guards and who carries."

Ohmigod, I think I broke something.

Dropping the box she carried with a loud *thump,* Nina reached around to massage her aching lower back. For the past hour, she'd toted boxes, more than she'd realized they had. Her kids had helped with some of the smaller items, but boxes of books, videos, clothes and toys were heavy, and Nina was seriously reconsidering whether she'd "won" the coin toss.

Wiping her forehead, she glanced at David. Seated on the ground, with one of her kids on either side of him and his legs stretched toward the curb, he laughed heartily at a story Izzy shared. Earlier he'd sent the kids down the block to pick up meatball subs from the Italian deli on the corner. Now the three of them sat with saucy submarine sandwiches on their laps and sodas by their knees, having a picnic. The rats.

She'd ditched her baseball cap when the wind had died down an hour ago, thank goodness, but now she was hot, sweaty and intermittently chilled. All because of a stupid coin toss.

No, all because you're too dang stubborn to accept help from a man when it's offered.

Ever since she'd agreed to take David's job, she'd been asserting her independence in other ways, like insisting she could handle the move on her own.

Bubby thought she was nuts, and obviously so did David, but they didn't understand.

Working at Hanson's had given her confidence when her husband had walked out on her. It had given her courage when Zach had been diagnosed with asthma: She could provide for his health care. She could count on herself. Relying on someone else—who might or might not be around for the long haul—was too scary.

Nina swiped moisture from the back of her neck. She was just a sweaty single mother trying to keep her head on straight. Trying to raise two healthy, well-adjusted young people in a world where inconsistency was the rule rather than the exception. She didn't want her children to believe that it was normal for people to walk in and out of each other's lives as easily as they changed shirts. She wanted them to experience stability, not loss. And as far as she could tell, maintaining her independence was the only way to accomplish that.

On the other hand, she'd been pretty independent so far today.

There were only a few boxes left, but she ached from head to toe.

And her stomach growled.

And she wanted a meatball.

Digging into her pocket, she pulled out a quarter and approached the lunch bunch.

"I'd like a rematch," she said to David, flipping the

coin in the air. "I think I've been very unfair, making you sit here, questioning your masculinity and all."

Leisurely he took a bite of his sandwich, chewed, swallowed and said, "No, I feel okay about that now."

She smiled. "Really? Because you look a little…insecure. Let's flip again. Heads I keep moving, tails you take over." She tossed the coin in the air before he could protest. Catching it mid-fly and slapping it on the back of her hand, she said, "Ah, look at that! Tails."

David raised a knee, rested his forearm atop it and eyed her. "And I can trust you on this?"

"Oh, absolutely." She pocketed the quarter.

He nodded toward his paper-wrapped lunch. "There's half of an excellent meatball sandwich here. Can I trust that it will still be there when I return?"

"I hate meatballs."

David stood, brushed off his jeans and gazed down at her. "I heard your stomach growl."

She sighed. "David, if we're going to work together, we're going to have to learn to trust each other, aren't we?"

"You don't need a root-beer float." Nina reached into the corners of the window she had just sprayed with glass cleaner and dug out the dust. "You just had lunch," she reminded David, who had finished packing the van and was now helping her and the kids clean the apartment so she could collect her security deposit.

David removed a long-deceased moth and a very crunchy spider from the inside of the living-room light fixture. Then he borrowed the glass cleaner to spritz the glass dome so it would be sparkling clean when he reattached it to the ceiling.

"Excuse me," he countered as he worked, "but *I* did not have my lunch. *You* had my lunch. And for the record, it's just wrong to lie about disliking meatballs."

"We're almost finished here. If you want, I'll make you meatballs for dinner." She sneezed. "I must be allergic to something in this cleaning fluid."

"Here." David took the paper towels. "You sweep the kitchen. I'll rehang this light and then finish the windows."

"We already swept the kitchen. And mopped. This is all that's left."

"Well, sit on the floor then and supervise."

Because she was exhausted, Nina didn't argue. She plopped onto the carpet, trusted that the kids were cleaning their rooms and watched David climb the step stool and stretch up to hang the light. As he reached, she could see his abdomen beneath his sweater. Nice. Flat and very nice.

He glanced down at her. "So, will you really make me meatballs?"

He sounded surprised, hopeful. As if the notion gave him some deep pleasure. She considered her aching body and, at the moment, equally aching head, and weighed that against his smile. "Yes, Mr. Hanson. I will make you meatballs."

Considering her answer as he screwed in the fixture, he smiled. "To tell the truth, I think I've had my fill of meatballs for the day, and I'm sure the kids have." He hopped down from the step stool. "Let's stop by the market on the way home, anyway, though, for essentials like ice cream. And chocolate sauce. I make a mean soda. It'll knock your socks off, Miss Baxter. We'll call it a housewarming party." He folded the step stool to carry to the van then asked, apparently as an afterthought, "Do you make lasagna?"

Nina had never been as devoted to cooking as Bubby. The domestic goddess gene has skipped her generation.

But she liked the way David said *the kids*.

And he moved boxes.

And he was going to make ice cream sodas.

And every time he was fed, he smiled like a big, happy cat.

"I make such good lasagna," she said, trying—and failing—to ignore the way his brows rose and his smile stretched slowly, pleasurably, across his face. *Aw, hell.* She smiled back. "I make garlic bread, too."

Chapter Seven

Within a half hour of moving their belongings into David's condominium, Izzy and Zach were able to make themselves right at home. They loved having their own rooms, exclaimed in joy over the spaciousness of the condo and the electronic amenities. It appeared to Nina that David had picked up a few items, too, since she'd been here last.

The library was now also David's office, while his former office had become a den, complete with a large plasma TV, DVD player, stereo system and PlayStation. A stunning assortment of age-appropriate DVDs and CDs filled a shelving unit. It would have taken most of Nina's salary for the next six months to pay for all those goodies.

There were changes in Nina's suite, too: candles and potpourri and bath salts from an expensive bed-and-bath boutique.

When they'd stopped at the market on the way "home"—a pit stop Nina had unsuccessfully tried to veto—David had made her stay outside with the van while he and the kids had descended on the gourmet market he liked best. They emerged with not merely the makings of a knock-your-socks-off ice-cream soda, but a bulging bag filled with treats from the gourmet deli.

It was 6:00 p.m. by the time all the boxes were stacked neatly in their respective rooms, the van was locked up tight for the night and everyone was ready for dinner. Nina's head was throbbing with more rhythm than a rap album, and she'd have been thrilled to try out the bath salts before pouring her aching body into bed. But there was business to attend to, namely the business of having a chat with two children who were sure they had just walked into paradise.

Before she accompanied Zach and Izzy to the kitchen to prepare their dinner, she sat them down on David's gorgeous leather sofa, where she immediately admonished them never, ever, ever to sit with food, drink or fountain pens. Then she got down to the serious stuff.

Content to have David safely ensconced in his office on a business call, Nina stood before her politely attentive children and began her this-is-how-we-behave-in-someone-else's-home spiel.

"Most everything in here is designed for adults, not kids," Nina warned, waving a hand to indicate the light carpeting and handblown glass bowls. "If we spill a soda or throw a ball in here—even a Nerf ball—we could wind up paying Mr. Hanson back for the rest of our natural lives. So no eating or playing in these rooms."

"Where do we eat?" Izzy asked.

"The kitchen. *Only* the kitchen."

"What about in the den in front of the TV?" Zach asked. "You're supposed to eat in dens. Teddy's mom says all his dad needs to be happy is a cheese steak, his den and a barking lounger."

"Barcalounger." Nina thought it over a moment. She loved popcorn and a weepy movie. That was how she spent most of her Saturday nights after the kids went to bed. But if she allowed popcorn then she'd have to allow sodas, and she hadn't missed the new chenille-covered love seat in David's former office. "No." She shook her head. "No food in the den. Sorry, buddy."

"We have to remember that I'm here to work. Mr. Hanson will be hosting business dinners. The house has to look good all the time, so we've got to make sure there's a place for everything and everything in its place."

Her children began to look positively horrified, which she decided wasn't an altogether bad thing. She was sure the plasma TV, PlayStation and giant-size bedrooms were planting ideas of permanence in their pre-teenage heads.

Five minutes later, her children's eyes were going glassy and their mouths were turning down at the edges. Nina pressed on with what she hoped were gentle but firm admonishments not to think of this as their home…because it wasn't.

"This is temporary," she stated, lowering her voice a bit. "We're here indefinitely, but only until I can find an appropriate permanent position and our own housing again. So it's important to treat this place the way you would treat, say, Mrs. Watson's house." She named one of Bubby's friends, who had a three-bedroom home in the suburbs and often invited the kids over to play in the yard.

"Mrs. Watson's house smells like mothballs." Izzy wrinkled her nose.

"And she serves broken cookies," Zach added. "Bubby says she buys them for half price at the bakery."

"But we can't tell what kind we're eating!" Izzy shook her head. "We don't like it there."

"All right." Trying to keep her cool, Nina held up a hand to stave off more complaints. "Maybe that wasn't a good example, but whether or not you like it isn't the point. The point is when you're a guest in someone's home, you treat it extra-carefully and with respect."

As if by magic, the mutinous pouts on her children's faces softened. Zach nodded broadly. Izzy looked at him and, taking his cue, nodded broadly also.

Nina used the glimmer of hope and satisfaction she felt to spur her on to a recitation of the house rules.

"If you want to use the telephone here, please ask me first. No friends over on nights when Mr. Hanson is entertaining, so you'll have to check with me first to get the schedule…."

As she continued, Zach and Izzy appeared alert and attentive, shaking or nodding their heads appropriately. They also, however, appeared to find much of what Nina said to be very humorous. Their mouths looked like someone had pulled too hard on drawstrings, a sure sign that they were trying not to laugh. When she saw Zach's gaze travel behind her, she became suspicious and glanced at the mirror above the sofa while she spoke.

David stood behind her, grinning and nodding ridiculously when she told the children what they could do; he frowned deeply and wagged an admonishing finger when she listed a behavior she wanted them to avoid.

"So if it's raining, no shoes on in the house, and *what are you doing?*" Whirling, she caught David mid-wag.

Izzy gasped dramatically and slapped a hand on her mouth. Zach giggled.

David grinned. "That's an awful lot of rules you've got there, Mom."

She blinked. He was criticizing her? He ought to be thanking her! "Pardon me," she said with great dignity and gravity. "I am trying to advise my children on how to behave in someone else's home."

"And I'm trying to make them feel at home. Can we have ice cream sodas now?"

The kids jumped up.

"No!" Nina held out a hand to stay them.

"Why not?"

"You were supposed to say, '*May* we,'" Zach prompted.

"Ohhh." David nodded. "May we have—"

"That is not why! No one is going anywhere until you've been excused."

"May we please be excused now?" Izzy piped up.

Exasperated, Nina flapped a hand at her children. "Yes, fine." She glared at David, who had decided to take Zach's place on the sofa. "What are you doing now?"

"I wasn't excused."

"There are no excuses for you, Mr. Hanson."

"You're right. None whatsoever. I apologize for my, may I say, uncharacteristically juvenile behavior." Then he leaned forward. "I'm having a great time. I realize you're uncomfortable with this situation, so pathetic confession number one—I never had kids of my own, and I was a workaholic when my nephews were young. Being around your kids—who make me laugh, by the way—gives me a chance to live vicariously. Pathetic confession number two." He clasped his hands. Refined, comforting hands. "The thought of filling my very large, very quiet home with the sound of other people works for me right now. Please don't ask your kids to be too quiet here, Nina. This place feels like a morgue sometimes."

Nina felt her resistance to the entire situation drop a notch. Every time she thought she'd shored up her immunity to David, he managed to touch her. Usually by saying something exquisitely simple.

"Is there a three?" she asked.

David cocked his head. "Three?"

"Is there a pathetic confession number three?"

"Ah." He shook his head. "No. Two per day is my limit. I don't like to overindulge." Standing, he smiled with no apparent agenda other than to enjoy the evening. "Except when it comes to ice cream. Time for sodas." He deferred to her with a nod. "All right?"

What could she do but nod in return?

"Good," he said, rubbing his palms together. "Stand back and let a master show you how it's done."

I think I just have, Nina thought, knowing already that making the decision to leave here would be more difficult than the decision to move in.

Despite a lingering headache and fatigue that she attributed to the move, Nina spent the following two

Play the

Lucky Hearts Game

and get...

2 FREE BOOKS
and a **FREE MYSTERY GIFT...**
YOURS to KEEP!

yes!

I have scratched off the silver card.
Please send me my *2 FREE BOOKS* and
FREE mystery GIFT. I understand that I am
under no obligation to purchase any books as
explained on the back of this card.

Scratch Here!
then look below to see
what your cards get you...
2 Free Books & a Free
Mystery Gift!

335 SDL EEX9   **235 SDL EEWX**

FIRST NAME   LAST NAME

ADDRESS

APT.#   CITY

STATE/PROV.   ZIP/POSTAL CODE   (S-SE-02/06)

Twenty-one gets you
2 FREE BOOKS
and a **FREE MYSTERY GIFT!**

Twenty gets you
2 FREE BOOKS!

Nineteen gets you
1 FREE BOOK!

TRY AGAIN!

The Silhouette Reader Service™ — Here's how it works:

Accepting your 2 free books and gift places you under no obligation to buy anything. You may keep the books and gift and return the shipping statement marked "cancel." If you do not cancel, about a month later we'll send you 6 additional books and bill you just $4.24 each in the U.S., or $4.99 each in Canada, plus 25¢ shipping & handling per book and applicable taxes if any.* That's the complete price and — compared to cover prices of $4.99 each in the U.S. and $5.99 each in Canada — it's quite a bargain! You may cancel at any time, but if you choose to continue, every month we'll send you 6 more books, which you may either purchase at the discount price or return to us and cancel your subscription.

*Terms and prices subject to change without notice. Sales tax applicable in N.Y. Canadian residents will be charged applicable provincial taxes and GST. Credit or debit balances in a customer's account(s) may be offset by any other outstanding balance owed by or to the customer.

If offer card is missing write to: The Silhouette Reader Service, 3010 Walden Ave., P.O. Box 1867, Buffalo, NY 14240-1867

BUSINESS REPLY MAIL

FIRST-CLASS MAIL   PERMIT NO. 717-003   BUFFALO, NY

POSTAGE WILL BE PAID BY ADDRESSEE

SILHOUETTE READER SERVICE
3010 WALDEN AVE
PO BOX 1867
BUFFALO NY 14240-9952

NO POSTAGE
NECESSARY
IF MAILED
IN THE
UNITED STATES

days organizing the library/office into a functional work space. David suggested she take a couple of days simply to settle in with her kids, but she ignored him. Her children were in electronics heaven, and she needed to focus on work in order to remind herself that their stay here was first, last and in between about business.

It didn't take too long for David to fall into step with her. They worked smoothly together, organizing files and compiling task lists. After the first couple of hours on Sunday, Nina noted a marked change in David's demeanor, however. He started out relaxed and casual, as he had been during the move, but by midday he was the David Hanson she knew from the office—polite, professional and remote.

On Monday she phoned him at the office to tell him about Zach's early-morning appointment with the pulmonary specialist. The visit had offered far more promise than their usual doctor appointments, and both she and Zach had left the office in good spirits. David picked up her call by saying, "Yes, Miss Baxter? What can I do for you?" Nina told herself that the distance, the return to formality—even to a bit of awkwardness between them—was right. It was good.

She worked furiously through Monday afternoon, keeping her mind on business, and by the time she picked her children up from school—a luxury afforded by the job's flexible hours—she was ready to collapse in the wondrously comfortable bed David had given her.

She was on day three of her headache, plus now her body protested every move and her throat was sore. Her children would have been thrilled with drive-through burgers or microwaved frozen dinners featuring a fat and sugar content guaranteed to accelerate the hardening of their arteries. Nina, however, insisted on preparing something fresh and reminiscent of the food pyramid while Zach and Izzy worked on homework at the kitchen counter.

She was sautéing broccoli and red peppers for a pasta sauce and concentrating hard on remaining upright when David arrived home.

He looked tired as he entered the kitchen, leaned against the counter and watched her. He remained like that, not speaking, simply watching her cook, a full minute. Then he straightened, raised a hand carrying a briefcase and pointed at her. "You should not be cooking. You look as if you're about to keel over."

"I'm fine, and good evening to you, too," she snapped, too sick and irritable to admit that he was right. "I'm making pasta. There's plenty if you're hungry."

Nina kept her pounding head lowered and was surprised when the large sauté spoon was plucked from her hand.

"Sit down," David commanded. "You look like

you're about to fall face first into the skillet. You're probably scaring your children."

Nina glanced toward her kids, who should have been studying, but instead were engaged in a discussion about gummy worms. Go figure. Nina smirked at David. "You don't know much about kids. Right now my children's biggest concern is their empty stomachs. Give me back the spoon."

He held it out of her reach. "You look like hell."

Nina's eyes widened, which hurt her head. Apparently their strictly business relationship was on a different footing after five.

Unable to argue the fact that she looked awful, she settled for logic. "You can't stir spaghetti sauce—you're wearing a white shirt." *Nyah, nyah, nyah.*

Reaching into a drawer, David withdrew a large dish towel and tucked it into his collar, letting it drape across his chest. He looked ridiculous. And certain that he'd won the argument. So she let him. Sort of.

At 7:00 p.m., after supervising dinner from a stool at the kitchen counter, Nina crawled into bed with a glass of water and two ibuprofen.

Zach and Izzy were with David, watching *Shrek 2* and laughing uproariously when Shrek passed wind.

Nina had had no idea—none, not a lick, not a clue—that David would be so eager—or that he would enjoy the kids so much. She'd had a very different scenario in mind when she'd finally agreed to move in.

Jerking the covers up on her luscious queen-size bed, she shivered beneath the duvet. She certainly would have stayed up and made sure the kids got into bed okay, but she was so achy she could hardly sit upright and her head was still pounding. David and the kids had urged her to call it a night, promising that bedtimes would be honored and no food would leave the kitchen area. Though David had moaned, "Aw, Mo-om," when she'd insisted on delivering the no-snacks-in-the-TV-room reminder.

Groaning a little from the effort, Nina reached up to turn off the bedside lamp. Apparently she was the only person in the house at present time who did not find this situation comfortable.

No, that wasn't true. It *was* comfortable. It was too comfortable. It was—

Tension filled her chest as she tried to block the word that came to mind.

Don't think it. Don't think it.

Perfect.

Arrrrghhhh!!! Nina grabbed a goose-down pillow, held it over her head and growled into it. David Hanson was a low-down, dirty double-crosser! The man was supposed to be a stiff-backed executive. He was supposed to socialize with models and socialites and other stiff-backed executives in swanky clubs and five-star restaurants. He was *not* supposed to enjoy whipping up ice-cream sodas or to laugh out loud at flatulent green ogres. If he was going to be so damned agreeable and easygoing, such a…such a…*family man,* then he ought to get his own family and leave single mothers with fantasy issues in peace.

Nina blew a long stream of air into the pillow. He was confusing her. She was getting all mixed up. There had been a moment in his kitchen that first night when he'd very carefully measured chocolate syrup into four glasses then just as carefully added soda. He'd kept lifting the glasses up, eyeballing them to make sure he had the perfect amounts of everything before he'd added his secret ingredient—a little shot of pure vanilla—and the tip of his tongue had rested on his lower lip as he'd concentrated. Nina had watched him, and in one unguarded second she'd thought to herself, *What a wonderful dad.*

She groaned again.

What a wonderful dad. That had to be the most dangerous thought a single mother could have about an unmarried man.

In the next second, in that kitchen, she'd wanted to kiss David Hanson. Right on the mouth. And then before she'd been able to preempt it, she'd had a vision of them all on a beach—her, Izzy, Zach and David—with Zach and Izzy racing ahead and her throwing her arms around David's neck while he picked her up and whirled her round and round on the sand. In the vision, everyone was laughing. Everyone was happy. Everyone was going to be together forever.

Help! She shook her head. Maybe she was feverish. She felt feverish.

"I've got to stop this train before there's a wreck," she said, her voice muffled by a three-hundred thread-count pillowcase. If she didn't slam the brakes on now, her next fantasy would feature Bubby baking the wedding cake.

She hadn't known she could still harbor such daydreams.

Feeling hotter and more claustrophobic by the second, she tossed the pillow aside and pushed her aching body to a sitting position. She didn't have her own apartment anymore; she couldn't leave now. But she could remind herself exactly why her life plan included her taking care of her family by herself and *excluded* inviting a man into the picture.

Sitting on the bed with the soft light of the bedside lamp creating a private ambience, Nina forced herself to go to the one feeling that could always remind her why she'd decided not to risk loving anyone new.

First she pictured faces, the perpetually smiling faces of her mother and father. Only in their thirties, in love with each other and their bright teenage daughter, they'd had every reason to smile. When Nina was fourteen, they'd gone on a second honeymoon. To welcome them home, Nina and Bubby had prepared a dinner that was the same meal they'd served at their wedding.

Sitting on the bed in David's house, Nina closed her eyes and remembered the anticipation, the excitement as she looked forward to their surprise and to sitting down with her mother to listen to the details of the trip.

"Marry a man whose hand you want to hold all your life," her mother would tell her as she always had when talking about the man she loved.

Nina had waited in the living room with Bubby, watching the clock. And watching. And watching. They hadn't been worried at first when her parents had been late. So many things could happen to delay an arrival from the airport. It had taken an hour and a half for Bubby to grow concerned enough to call the airline.

Remember. Remember, Nina commanded herself as she slipped back into the heart of the girl who in an instant had lost the safety and joy she had known. Still, though losing her parents in a plane crash had been devastating, that wasn't what had convinced her to stop inviting people into her life.

From fourteen to twenty-two, she had kept her heart open. Sometimes she'd thought it was her dreams that had saved her: the dreams of creating an intact family again, of recapturing the incomparable warmth of two parents and kids and wanting to hold someone's hand all your life.

She'd been so ready to be married at eighteen. Ready to have two babies at an age when most young women were still in college.

She had not been prepared to raise her children on her own. The end of the dream had felt like the loss of her parents all over again. In some ways it had been worse. For a long while she had found herself more lost, more depressed than before.

It was the depression that had truly frightened her. With two babies and a full-time job, she couldn't afford not to get out of bed in the morning. Thank heavens she'd used her insurance and her lunch hour to get counseling. A sage therapist had taught her that she'd never completely grieved for her parents. That she'd used her dreams to keep them alive and to avoid the deep-down fear that she was somehow destined to be alone.

So Nina had worked on grieving. When she hadn't been at work and when the kids had been in bed, she'd grieved. Slowly, she'd begun to feel better—lighter, more able to stand on her own and to jump into her life feet first.

It had taken only one additional failed romance to convince her absolutely that she would never put her kids through unnecessary pain and loss. Zach and Izzy and she, too, were happy as they were. Why mess with success? Why hand your contentment over to somebody else for safekeeping?

Nina rubbed her face. She was bone-tired. Really beat. But she was cognizant enough to know that the odds against a forty-four-year-old, never-married executive becoming a devoted family man—to a ready-made family, no less—were pretty steep. David was merely trying it on for size, the way he'd try on a new suit by the latest designer.

Well, if he wanted to experiment, fine and dandy. But by damn he could do it with someone else's kids, someone else's life.

Reaching for her pillow, she punched it several times then stuffed it once more behind her head and sighed as she leaned back. Their location may have changed, but she was still in charge. Come tomorrow, she'd show David Hanson who was the boss.

Chapter Eight

I'm dying.

Nina strained her neck to raise her aching head and peer at the clock. It read 7:15 a.m. Tuesday, if she recalled correctly.

"Nnnnnghhhhhmmmmph." Letting her head fall back against the pillow, she scanned her body for any part that *didn't* hurt.

Right pinkie, she thought. *Concentrate on your right pinkie.* The old focusing trick usually worked to help her overcome any physical discomfort enough to get moving, but not today. Today the mere thought of being upright made her want to weep.

She had the flu, no doubt about it. Her head was

pounding, she felt cold and hot at the same time, she was queasy; even her eyeballs and her teeth ached.

She seriously considered lying in bed indefinitely, but her children's voices roused her attention. She heard Zach laughing, and Izzy saying, "More! More!"

They sounded too far away to be in one of the bedrooms. When Nina imagined them preparing their own breakfasts in David's pristine kitchen, she heaved herself out of bed and pictured every cell in her body holding a protest sign.

Moving with care, she pulled a robe on over her T-shirt and pajama bottoms then tucked her feet into clogs. She clumped heavily to the bathroom, where she brushed her teeth and scraped her curls into an exploding ponytail. Apologizing to her reflection, she promised herself an open account at Victoria's Secret in her next life.

She hauled herself to the kitchen, expecting to see her children alone, pouring more cereal than any two people could consume in one sitting. Instead, she found both her kids teaching David how to make a tablespoon stick to his nose.

"Rub harder," Zach instructed. "You've gotta make the spoon feel hot."

"Okay, now!" Izzy crowed. "See if it'll stick now!"

Obedient to her children's commands, David let the bowl of a shiny tablespoon rest on his nose, where it held a few moments before it dropped. Laughter filled the kitchen.

"I think that's the first time I ever had a spoon on my nose." David grinned.

"Have you ever put straws up it?" Izzy asked quite seriously.

"Why would I do that?"

"You do it to look like a walrus." She shrugged. "Little kids like it."

"Hmm. I don't think I have any straws."

"Lucky you." When Nina spoke, the words emerged like a strange croak. The threesome in the kitchen turned to look at her.

"Did we wake you up?" David asked, an apologetic expression on his perfectly shaved, perfectly handsome face.

Nina tugged on the belt of her robe, acutely aware that she was the only person present who was not dressed and ready for the day. Not a good way to impress the boss.

Though a mighty fine reason why you shouldn't live with him in the first place.

"I'm usually up every morning by six," Nina said. "I don't know why my alarm didn't go off."

"David said we should let you rest, so me and Zach sneaked in and turned it off!" Izzy beamed, proud of herself and her brother.

David held up his hands when Nina glanced at him. "The alarm wasn't my idea. Although I think it was a good one. You looked a little done in yesterday."

Well, that was good to know.

"Are you all right this morning?" he asked, his doubtful expression telegraphing clearly the fact that she didn't look any better today.

"I may be coming down with something," Nina admitted reluctantly. "But I'll be fine in a couple of hours. I'll take some zinc." Self-consciously she glanced at her outfit. "I would have dressed, but I wanted to get the kids' breakfast."

On her last word, the toaster popped up.

"Got that covered." David grabbed two plates. "Toaster waffles." He raised a brow. "Is that okay?"

In response, she sneezed. Messily.

"Oooh, gross, Mommy!" Izzy covered her eyes.

Quickly, Nina grabbed a napkin from a Lucite holder on the counter.

"Cool." Zach grinned. "We studied mucus in science class. When you have a cold, the human body can produce a cup of mucus." He looked at David. "How much do you think she sneezed out?"

With a hand at the back of Zach's head, David guided the young scientist to a stool at the breakfast bar. "I think we have more to look forward to."

Zach was in high spirits since his visit with the pulmonary specialist. The doctor took a variety of approaches to asthma, and he was confident that Zach would be able to manage his condition without increased steroids. He'd even told the boy that one of his asthma patients was now a pro baseball player. Zach had excitedly told David the news last night, and David had promised Zach a trip to Wrigley Field, an offer that catapulted him to hero status.

Nina blew her nose and eyed her children's new best friend over the Kleenex.

Meeting her eyes, David asked, "Are you hungry?"

She surveyed the granite counter, set with butter and syrup for the waffles, orange juice and milk. Her sore throat protested at the thought of a single swallow. "Are you eating?" she said, wishing for a throat lozenge.

"I'm an oatmeal man in the morning." He shook his head woefully. "Ever since I turned forty, health has taken precedence over taste. You're lucky." He looked at her with a smile, as if her present appearance were perfectly normal and perfectly attractive. "You don't have to worry about age yet."

"You're *forty years old?*" Izzy exclaimed, blatantly disturbed by the news. "That's almost as old as our principal."

"No it's not!" Zach piped up, rolling his eyes at his sister. "Mr. Kenner's hair is white already. He's probably fifty."

"Well, I hate to break it to you both," David confessed, "but I'm forty-four."

Izzy looked at David as if she were profoundly depressed. "Then you'll probably never get married. Bubby says if a man isn't married by the time he's thirty-five he's either a miser or a schmuck."

"Isabella!" Nina gave her daughter the "angry eyeball," as her children liked to call her best parental glare. The next time she saw her grandmother, Bubby was going to get a dose of the angry eyeball, too.

"Don't worry, David, plenty of old guys get married." Zach spoke with the confidence of a true authority on the subject. "They even have babies. It's old women who don't get married."

"Zach!" For the first time in memory, Nina wanted to stuff a sock in her son's mouth. She sneezed again, blew her nose and apologized to David. "Obviously my children have been watching too much MTV. They're having trouble recognizing that anyone over twenty-five is still breathing, much less capable of having a social life."

Zach looked sheepish. "Sorry, Mom." He lowered his head to his orange juice. "I didn't mean you, exactly."

Izzy spoke while painstakingly pouring syrup into each indentation of her waffle. "You're not old, Mom. You're just stressed because you're single. But you could still get married." When her waffle was filled to capacity, she looked up with a smile meant to be encouraging. "You might even still be able to have babies. But you'll probably need fertilizer treatments, and you could wind up with twins like Rachel Abrams's mom, and then you'll think you ought to have your head examined."

"Oh, my God," Nina said, blushing furiously.

David turned around, rested both palms on the

granite countertop, hung his head and laughed so hard his shoulders shook.

Izzy grumbled, "What's so funny?" Zach shrugged, and they both started eating, avoiding their mother's gaze.

"Go ahead and enjoy yourself, Methuselah." Nina croaked to David above his laughter. "You won't think it's so funny if Viagra is taken off the market."

He sobered immediately. "Have you heard Viagra's being taken off the market? Are there rumors on the Internet?" When Nina laughed, he grinned. "I'll make a deal with you, Nina. I'll keep my ear to the ground for a good deal on fertilizer, and you inform me of any Viagra sales that come to your attention."

Nina nodded. "Deal. I suppose those of us who have a foot in the grave ought to stick together."

His grin eased to a relaxed smile. "My thoughts exactly. So, how about it, Mrs. Dorian Gray? Want to gum some oatmeal with me?"

Nina looked at her children, who listened avidly to the conversation while they ate. "I want to take a shower," she said, "and a couple of aspirin before I eat anything. And I need to drive the kids to school."

"Got that covered, too," David said. "I'll drive them."

"What?" A caring, responsible man who was not her husband, father or brother was offering to take her children to school…after making them breakfast so she could sleep in? The data entered Nina's brain, but wouldn't immediately compute. "No, I couldn't possibly... I mean, thank you, but—"

"Please, Mom?" Zach leaned so far over his plate, his shirt touched his waffle. "David's car is sweet! No one's *ever* come to school in a Mustang!"

"Mr. Hanson's car is not the issue. Get your shirt out of the syrup." She turned to David. "You have to go to work."

"I'll drop them off on my way to the office."

"Their school isn't on your way."

David sighed. "This is going to be one of those annoying conversations that we have. Isn't it?"

She wasn't sure how to respond to that.

"You may as well give in now, Nina. I'm definitely driving them. You're definitely staying home. They'll get to school safe and on time. Scout's honor."

"I don't know—"

"Mo-o-om!" Izzy joined Zach's plea.

David arched a brow and Nina sniffed. "I suppose I could use the extra time to compile a list of caterers. I want to call and get price lists—"

"Give it a rest, Miss Baxter. Literally."

"I'm not that sick. I'd rather get right to work. I—" Closing her eyes, she sneezed into her paper napkin. Loudly. Messily.

"Ooooh, gross!" This time David made the comment, and Zach and Izzy laughed around mouthfuls of waffle.

"Fine, go," Nina said after blowing her nose again. "I'll be able to sneeze in peace."

Zach and Izzy immediately began arguing over who got to sit in the Mustang's front seat.

"Have fun," she said, grabbing several more napkins off the counter and giving her children a little wave. "Come to my room before you go, and I'll give you lunch money. Zach, make sure you take your inhaler."

"Maybe he should leave it for you," David cracked. "You really do sound sick. I'll check back with you."

"No, no," she insisted, shuffling toward her room. "I'm fine. I'm going to take a shower. You three have fun— *Ahhh-chew!*"

Nina got into the tub after she left David and the kids. She decided that a hot soak would ease her sore muscles and wake her up, but an hour later she awoke in a cold tub with muscles that ached more than ever and pounding temples that required additional pain-killers. When she emerged from the bath, even her toes hurt, so she donned her soft chenille robe and swallowed two more ibuprofen.

While she'd been soaking, David had phoned and left a message, asking how she was. Nina had called back, but he'd been in a meeting, so she'd asked his secretary to tell him that she felt much better and thanks for everything. Then she'd crawled into bed for a few minutes…just a few…to finish the nap she'd started in the bath.

That's where David found her several hours later, after clearing his afternoon and leaving her another message to say he intended to pick the kids up from school and take them to the zoo for a couple of hours so she could continue to rest. Just to get a rise out of her, he added that he hoped she really was resting, but that given her obstinate nature, he figured there was a fifty-fifty chance she was out tarring the roof.

At the zoo, outgoing Izzy had waved her hand madly when a performer at the live animal show had requested parent-and-child volunteers. "We can pretend," she'd whispered to David when they'd been chosen. Close together onstage, they had held out their arms so a trained owl could land on them. Izzy had squealed, and David had used his free arm to hold her steady. The owl had cocked its head and blinked, and the audience had cheered. The staff performer had said that David and Izzy made a great team, which had made Izzy smile so widely, David was sure the entire audience had been able to see her molars.

The funny thing was, something inside him felt like it was beaming just as broadly. He'd spent most of his adult life keeping his distance from people, either by design or by circumstance. He'd had some initial concern that Zack and Izzy might become bored with his company. What did he know about entertaining kids, after all? He'd hardly ever been one. But they'd liked having him around, and he liked knowing that.

It had been the most satisfying couple of hours he'd spent in years.

On the way home, he'd found himself mentally planning a trip to the children's museum until he'd pulled on the reins and told himself to slow down. Way down. He needed time to digest the unfamiliar feelings before he waded farther into this particular pool. Yes, he'd invited—all right, pressured—Nina to move herself and her children into his home, but how far they moved into his life was still up to him.

So when he returned to the apartment, he intended to tell Nina they'd had a good time at the zoo. That's it. Just a simple, "Yes, we had a good time," and leave it at that. But the kids ran directly to their mother's room and returned to report that she was sleeping again.

"She sounds like she's got asthma, like me," Zach said. He and Izzy stared at David as if they expected him to take some action.

"Maybe we should call Bubby," Izzy prompted.

"I think we should go in and look at her again," Zach said.

"I think your mother has a cold or maybe the flu and that she needs her rest. You're probably not used to seeing her rest much, are you?"

"I want to go look at her again." Izzy started toward the bedroom.

David tugged the hood of her sweatshirt to keep her in the living room. "I'm not sure that's a good idea."

He guessed the girl was going to awaken her mother in order to reassure herself. In all likelihood this was the first time Nina had gotten time off from her life.

"But Zach says she's breathing funny."

While two pairs of wide, worried eyes applied as much pressure as a boardroom full of investors, David tried to balance reason with caution.

Izzy was used to seeing her brother struggle for air; she knew the result was sometimes serious. It was natural for her to feel more fear than the situation warranted.

David asked himself what he would do right now, what his immediate response would be if Nina Baxter were his personal concern, not only his personal assistant.

I'd watch over her and make sure she knew she could rest without worrying—about the kids, about health insurance, about anything.

…And while she lay in bed, trying to sleep off her cold, he would stroke her forehead, her cheeks, the bridge of her nose. He would brush back her hair and when she felt well enough, he'd wash it for her in the kitchen sink….

He swiped a hand down his face. *Get a grip, man.*

"All right, I'll go look at her," he said, feeling and sounding gruff. Zach and Izzy immediately nodded. "I'm not going to wake her up, though," he cautioned. "I'll listen to her breathing, and if she needs a doctor, we'll call one. All right?"

Solemnly, the children nodded again.

"Good. You two get started on your homework. I'll check on your mom, and then we'll figure out something for dinner."

As he headed down the hall, he thought he sounded like a man who had everything under control. That was good PR.

When he reached Nina's bedroom, he pushed on the slightly open door and edged into the room. With the curtains closed, the bedroom was cool and dim. A slice of light from the hallway provided the majority of illumination. Moving gingerly toward the bed, he could see Nina asleep on her back, several scrunched tissues around her head and clutched in her hands.

She was snoring—due, he hoped, to congestion. Her mouth was open; a little rivulet of drool shone in the light. Her masses of curly blond hair were spread across the pillow, reminding him less of a romantic silk waterfall and more of lots and lots of unraveled yarn. Soft yarn.

While he watched her, she appeared to have an attack of sleep apnea. Her head jerked and a loud snort escaped. David jumped back when she started to awaken. Thankfully, she dropped against the pillow again…with several more snorts. She licked her lips, brushed at the drool with the back of her hand then groaned, turned away from him and settled once again into a nice snore.

David felt his frowning brow relax. An odd tightness in his chest eased, and he began to laugh. Silently, but so hard he knew he had to get out of the room quickly.

Creeping out and down the hall the same way he'd crept in, he slipped into his library, closed the door, sat at his desk and let the laughter come until he actually felt tears at the corners of his eyes.

He'd been all over the world, had dated women who shared his background and his lifestyle. Women, who, it had seemed, managed never to have an unattractive moment. Women whose unencumbered lives had allowed him to come and go as he'd pleased.

With all her personal commitments, the baggage Nina would bring to a relationship could fill a moving van. In only a few weeks of knowing her on more than a superficial level, he'd discovered that she was stubborn, always put her family first, had spent more time in senior centers than nightclubs and sneezed louder than any of the men in his college fraternity.

David wiped his eyes and sighed. For a second there in the bedroom, he'd seen his life as it would look with Nina rather than with the type of women he usually dated.

Yes, he'd gotten a good laugh out of that. But what had really struck his funny bone was the realization that in forty-four years, he'd never once thought of wiping someone else's runny nose or of kissing them while they drooled.

Until now.

Chapter Nine

"I'b weady to wook, I tell you."

"No, you're not."

Nina heard paper shuffling on the other end of the phone she held to her ear with one hand while she jammed Kleenex to her nose with the other.

She had only vague memories of last night. Mostly she remembered being so fatigued that she'd awakened only enough to open her eyes, utter a token protest when David had fed her canned soup and NyQuil, and then close her eyes again and pretend to be asleep already while he'd cupped a palm over her brow to check for fever.

Oh, that palm. Cool and large and immensely

comforting. Drifting in and out of a restless sleep, Nina had sensed someone beside her for what had seemed like a long, long time. It could have been delirium, but her impression was that David had stayed with her for a couple of hours.

Then today she'd dragged her protesting body out of bed at seven to make the kids' lunches and to drive them to school, only to find that David had helped them make their own lunches the night before and had gotten them up early so they could eat breakfast out before, once again, *he* dropped them off at school. They'd all signed a card to her, wishing her a nice, quiet day of rest.

For the first time in years, Nina had felt no need to be in control. She had been the cared for, not the caretaker.

Any single mother with half a brain—make that one tenth of a brain—would have spent the entire day moving from the bed to the jetted tub and back again. She'd have allowed herself a few delicious fantasies about the boss and would have phoned her girlfriends—from the tub—to say, "You are not going to believe the situation I've landed in."

So what had Nina done? She'd read the note, sneezed five times in a row and cried into her tissue because she felt obsolete. Obsolete! It was ridiculous, but she was used to taking care of everything herself, of being the only adult in the family. She was used to feeling, basically, alone. Being taken care of had felt so odd and so good that this morning she was completely off balance and scared. She wanted to find normal again.

So she'd given David time to get to the office and then she'd phoned him to say she wanted to get to work.

David's mellow voice countered that notion. "You'll be of more help if you take the next few days to recuperate. There'll be plenty to do after that."

Nina tried to rise above her congestion. "I peel pine *now*. I cabe hewe to wook and dat's what I'b going to do!"

"To someone, somewhere I'm sure that makes sense." A smile lurked in David's wry voice. After he shuffled more papers, he said, "My housekeeper's name is Johanna. She'll be there at ten. If you need anything, ask her. In the meantime— Wait a sec." He covered the mouthpiece, spoke to someone then returned to Nina. "I've got to take a call from Japan. Relax and concentrate your energy on recuperating, Miss Baxter, not on becoming Secretary of the Year. In good time I expect you to rise like a phoenix and give new meaning to the word *vibrant*."

Nina could say nothing for a moment, then in a small voice she halfheartedly complained, "Dobody talks like dat."

"Rex Harrison did."

"Sixty years ago."

David chuckled. "I'll call you later."

The line went dead, but the phone in Nina's hand felt alive. *Vibrant?* Was that how he saw her?

Stop.

She set the phone in its cradle and blew her nose. Standing in the kitchen, she checked her reflection in the glass door of the double oven. She felt weepy and lost and tragic, not vibrant. At least she'd dressed as if she were going to work today—sky-blue blouse, navy skirt and pumps. Her hair was more or less tamed into a bun. In other words, all suited up to sit on the bench.

She wasn't used to staying home with nothing to do and too much to think about. In all her years at Hanson's she'd only used, max, a dozen sick days, and those had been for her kids, not her.

Nina started a coughing jag that had her rummaging through her pockets for the menthol lozenges she'd stashed there. Popping one into her mouth, she pushed it around with her tongue and made a plan.

First, she needed some cold medicine to de-fuzz her brain and decongest her nose. Then she'd call Judy Denton, David's administrative assistant at the office, and ask her what kind of errands, etc., David usually required. And, given the extra work created by layoffs, an offer of help with word processing would surely come as a welcome surprise.

Buoyed by the prospect of an active day to keep her mind busy, she crunched the throat lozenge to get it out of the way, picked up the phone and dialed

Hanson Media again. She'd show David Hanson who needed taking care of around here.

By 10:00 a.m., Nina had returned from the drugstore and taken a decongestant so she wouldn't sound like Elmer Fudd the rest of the day. Judy Denton had proved intractable when it came to sharing her boss's itinerary with anyone, including his new—and still nasal—personal assistant. Her advice to Nina? "It sounds as if you should rest, dear. I'm sure Mr. Hanson will give you directives soon."

Nina wasn't sure about directives, but she had an expletive or two she wanted to try out. She was standing at the door to his home office, chewing on a fingernail and seriously considering the merits of snooping for something to do, when she heard a key in the front door lock.

Jumping at the sound, she trotted to the foyer as a fifty-something woman in a trench coat entered the condominium.

Ice blue eyes raked Nina with out-and-out unfriendliness before a crisp voice with a decidedly British snap said, "I always let myself in. Are you all right with that?" The tone suggested that if Nina happened not to be all right with that, David would soon be looking for a new housekeeper.

"Fine," Nina said. "That's fine." She'd already forgotten about Johanna, the woman who came weekly to clean David's former bachelor-only abode.

Johanna was a tall, handsome woman with skin like ivory linen, gray hair cut close to her head and strong features. Her greeting suggested that she wasn't surprised to see Nina in the apartment. Her expression suggested she wasn't happy about it.

Nina thrust out her hand, realized she was still holding a crumpled, germ-ridden tissue and pulled back. "Hello, I'm Nina," she said, foregoing the handshake, "Dav— Mr. Hanson's personal assistant. I'll be living here with my children."

A thin brow arched to telling heights while Johanna's voice dropped to a telling low. "I heard."

She stomped a few steps past Nina then turned with obvious reluctance. "I suppose now's as good a time as any to get things straight. I clean for Mr. Hanson. Sometimes I cook. *For…Mr.…Hanson.* If he's got leftovers it's his business what he does with them. I don't take requests, so don't leave me any notes telling me your children like pasta and cheese."

Nina thought the most politic response would be a simple *okay*, but her throat chose that moment to tickle her violently, so she wound up nodding spasmodically while coughing.

Florence Nightingale she wasn't, but evidently even the unyielding Johanna felt some compassion for the ill. "Nasty cough," she said, shaking her head. "I'll fix that." Before she marched to the kitchen she issued a clear order. "You stay here. I don't want you spreading germs in my kitchen. I'll bring it when it's done."

Nina did not dare ask, of course, what "it" was. She considered herself fortunate that Johanna was willing to let her stay in the house.

"Oy vey," she sighed when the coughing jag was spent. Her boss refused to tell her what to do, and the housekeeper couldn't wait.

Maybe she should have spent the day in bed when she'd had the cha—

The doorbell jolted her away from the wall. She hurried to the door. Surprise flared when Bubby pushed past her into the foyer.

"My granddaughter is dying, and she doesn't even call me." Weighed down by two paper-handled grocery bags, Bubby swept her head broadly from side to side. "That's what I get for minding my own business—silence. Secrets! *Oy,* what can I do?"

"Bubby." Nina knew better than to relieve Bubby of her burdens; she wasn't finished carrying them yet. Shutting the door, she trailed her grandmother into the living room. "I wasn't expecting you."

"Some news flash, Barbara Walters. You didn't give me the address, so why would you expect me?" Bubby stood with her back to Nina while she studied the unfamiliar living room. "Fancy," she proclaimed. Setting the paper bags on the floor with a thump, she turned to eagle-eye Nina. "A couple of days I figured I'd give you to settle in. I don't like to butt in."

"You know I never think you're butting in—"

"Imagine my surprise when I get a call first thing

this morning from David Hanson, who tells me, 'Good morning. Your granddaughter is on her deathbed.'"

"I am not on my deathbed! He didn't say that." Then Nina realized the really important part of Bubby's statement. "He called you?"

"Why not? I've got a phone." Bubby arched a sparse gray brow. "Have *you* got a phone?"

Point made. "I'm sorry. Everything was so hectic here. I thought I'd settle in first and then I'd call—"

Bubby raised her hands. "I don't want anyone to feel bad. You know that crazy Sylvia Cohen? *She* loves to make people feel guilty. Me, I'd rather mind my own business. Who's in the kitchen?"

Nina heard dishware clanking. "That's Johanna," she said sotto voce. "David's housekeeper."

"She's cooking?" The microwave beeped several times. "What is that? What's that smell?" The wrinkle of Bubby's nose suggested she found the aroma only marginally better than something that had been dead for a long time. Nina sniffed the air. It did smell a bit like boiled roadkill.

"Don't say anything," Nina whispered. "She's making something for my cough." Although Nina hoped to heaven that the thing she smelled was not it.

When Bubby heard that someone else was preparing cold remedies for *her* granddaughter, nothing short of a police barricade would have kept her out of the kitchen. Nina knew she'd said the wrong thing when her diminutive grandmother picked up her shopping bags and marched toward battle like General Patton.

Bubby was tough, but Johanna was bigger and knew where the kitchen knives were stored. "Bubby, wait!" She started after her grandmother, but the doorbell rang. "Company!" she singsonged, trying to motion Bubby back. "Company!"

Bubby kept marching. Torn, Nina raced first to the door, flinging it open to a young man who carried a box filled with, from what Nina could tell, plastic containers of food.

"Hi," he said, "I'm from Ciao Chow's. I have a home delivery for Mr. Hanson."

"Oh!" Ciao Chow's was a popular gourmet food mart featuring a deli that offered the best pasta take-out in town.

Bemused, Nina wondered whether to take the box, referee the meeting in the kitchen or run for her purse to get money for a tip. Before she could debate the merits of each option, the hall elevator opened to emit a tall, willow-thin redhead in a dress as brightly pink as a begonia.

Samantha Edwards strode to the door with her customary intrepid stride. She smiled at the delivery boy, glanced in the box he carried and said, "Pasta! Yum!" Grinning at Nina, she held up a paper bag bearing the name of a local health-food store. "David told Jack you were sick. I brought herbs. We'll have you cured in no time!"

Chapter Ten

Apparently David thought Nina might need company.

So, he'd called Bubby, then he'd asked Jack if Samantha would mind paying Nina a visit, maybe bringing a few of the health supplements she poured down Jack. Then he'd called Ciao Chow's and told them to deliver so Nina wouldn't have to worry about food for the day.

She had to grin when Samantha explained the situation. David had sent her a Jewish grandmother *and* lunch? Boy, did he have a lot to learn. Still, she was...

Touched. Grateful. Very.

Now Bubby and Johanna were both in the kitchen,

striking an uneasy truce, or perhaps playing out their own version of *Iron Chef* as each prepared the one and only true cold remedy.

Samantha had seated herself on the living room couch and was pawing through her bag of supplements and homeopathic remedies.

"I was so surprised when David said he'd hired you and that you were living with him. You've been here—what, a few days now?" Her earrings—a row of flowers and leaves dangling from a long gold vine—swayed as she shook her head. "He's so solitary. You know this is the first time I've been to his place?"

Nina shook her head. She hadn't been acquainted with Samantha long before the layoffs and knew little about the other woman save for the fact that she was dynamic, creative, a strong businesswoman and in love with David's nephew, current CEO Jack Hanson. Samantha and Jack couldn't be more different, but their relationship appeared to work.

"The Hansons never seemed particularly…close," Nina said, treading onto territory she would have avoided had she still been working at the office. "It was nice to see Jack step in and work with David after George died. And they seem to get along."

"Jack respects David," Samantha agreed, examining a bottle of zinc-and-elderberry lozenges. "Although you're right. The Hansons aren't as tight as other families. I know Jack is working harder than he should have to in order to persuade his brothers to come home for the reading of George's will."

Unscrewing the lid on the zinc tabs, Samantha shook two lavender-colored lozenges into Nina's hand. "Let them dissolve in your mouth, one right after the other. Fact is," she said, recapping the bottle, "Jack would love to pass some of the responsibility for Hanson Media over to Andrew—he's the younger Hanson bro. Have you met him?"

Nina frowned, but in thirteen years with the company, she couldn't recall meeting Andrew. George hadn't been the kind of father who brought his sons to work with him. She shook her head.

"Well, Jack can barely get Andrew to return a phone call these days. He's pretty ticked. I think David's going to lay down the law about the reading of the will. Demand that all the boys haul their handsome Hanson tushies home."

Nina smiled. She liked the way Samantha talked. Popping a lozenge in her mouth, she quivered at the first tart taste then spoke around it. "Do all the Hansons have 'handsome tushies'?"

Samantha's smile turned mischievous. "I can certainly vouch for Jack's." She tilted her head. "David's too, come to think of it."

Nina's eyes bugged wide, and Samantha winked. "Fully clothed, fully clothed." She wagged a finger. "Shame on you. Although I must say if I were living with him I'd make sure to take at least a little peek."

Nina almost swallowed the lozenge whole. She started coughing and felt her face flame at the same time. Samantha reached over to wallop her on the back. For a reed-slender woman, she had quite a punch.

"Are you all right?" The outspoken executive appeared a bit worried for the first time today.

Nina pressed one hand to the base of her throat and used the other to wave away Samantha's concern. "Fine," she rasped. She pointed to her neck. "Piece of the lozenge…went down the wrong way."

"Ah." Samantha shrugged. She allowed thirty seconds of silence then said, "I can be a little too plain-spoken, or so I've been told. At the risk of not being able to walk out of here because I have both feet in my mouth, let me state for the record that when David told us he'd hired you to be his personal assistant and that you were living with him, Jack and I thought maybe you two had a *thing* going."

Nina opened her mouth immediately to refute that notion, but she started coughing again. Samantha hastened to add, "David set everyone straight. He said the setup between you two is strictly business."

Nina's mouth went so dry, the lozenge felt like it was super-glued to her tongue. "Yeth," she lisped around it, "thtrickly bithneth. Thtrickly." She tried to work a little moisture back into her mouth. "What do you mean 'everyone'?"

Samantha looked uncomfortable. "Oh, no. I meant *a few people*…in the boardroom. Shiguro Taka is coming to town—are you familiar with Taka Enterprises?—and David's going to do a little entertaining, so he mentioned at the meeting this morning that he'd hired you to help out with that." She handed Nina a bottle of chewable Cs. "And about how helpful it'll be to have you and your kids living in the condo, too, because Shiguro's wife and children will be coming with him. That's all."

Samantha futzed with the homeopathic remedy in her hands, twisting the cap to see how many pellets emerged at once. "There were only three…maybe four…I think six of us, not counting me and Jack, who heard him say it. It's no biggie."

"Eight people? He announced to eight people that I'm living with him? Oh, my God! Does the entire office think David and I are having an affair?"

"No, no!" Samantha shook her head vehemently. "Not anymore." She gave Nina's knee a reassuring pat. "I told you. David set the record straight."

She handed Nina the homeopathic remedy. "Follow the directions on this. But wait thirty minutes after the lozenge has dissolved before you take it." Rising, Samantha glanced toward the kitchen. "Something's starting to smell good. I'm sorry I have to go."

Nina rose, too, and the two women walked to the door. "I'd love to get together sometime when you're well and settled in here," Samantha added graciously before she left. "I've been trying my hand at cooking. Nothing fancy." She frowned. "The lasagna I made the other night was a little…crisp. Maybe I'll try a quiche, and we can brainstorm a few creative parties to woo the press. Hanson's could use a little lighthearted PR."

Nina agreed, thanked Samantha for the cold remedies and shut the door. Her head was beginning to feel fuzzy and overly full again, but she wasn't sure that was due to her cold.

Plopping on the couch, Nina realized she still had a zinc tablet in her hand. She set it on the coffee table and curled up on her side.

Holy moly, she was shaking, and something told her she didn't have the chills.

The conversation with Samantha replayed in her head.

What had shocked her was not so much Samantha's comments as her own reaction. What Nina had realized immediately was that she *wanted* to take a peek—just a tiny, quick one—at David's tush.

Curling into a tighter ball, she buried her face in her hands.

Yep, even now she felt an as-of-late unfamiliar warmth spread through her body when she imagined viewing David's nude backside. His nude shoulders, back and legs featured themselves prominently in the fantasy, too.

She rolled to her back and stared at the ceiling. When she pictured David showing up at her apart-

ment and at the hospital and at the senior center...
when she imagined his gaze, so steady, so penetrat-
ing...and when she realized that he thought of her
even when she wasn't in sight, she wondered if another man had *ever* made her feel that...held.

She released a shuddering sigh. Long ago she had
decided that being a good mother meant putting her
sexual and romantic needs on hold until her children
were grown and less likely to be affected by her
choices. She'd promised herself she would wear
white cotton underwear and avoid dating until her
children were twenty.

Was it wrong to change her mind in the course of a
morning? To know suddenly that she had missed love-
making? That she had missed *feeling loved* by a man?

Was it wrong to want sex with David so she could
discover if making love was different in the arms of
someone who knew how to care *for* a woman, not
merely about her?

Because David's bedroom suite was on the opposite end of the condo, a tryst or two would also be fairly
convenient. They could get together when the kids
weren't even home, and no one would be the wiser.

Nina wrapped her arms around herself. *This is what
happened when your mind was idle.* It was all hypo-
thetical, of course. She wasn't even close to making a
decision of such magnitude. But she did wonder....

Now that David had defended her honor, would
he mind very much besmirching it a little?

* * *

Dimly, as if from very far away, Nina heard someone snore. Because she was perfectly comfortable for the first time in days and because she was having a lovely dream in which she was naked with no cellulite on a tropical island, she ignored the sound.

Instead, she felt her lips curve at the edges as an equally nude David Hanson licked her sun-kissed shoulder. It tickled. All over.

"She must be dreaming."

"I'm going to have to make a potato poultice. She'll have a crick in her neck when she wakes up."

"Potato poultice. Does that work?"

"Of course."

Nina's brow puckered. The Yiddish and British-inflected conversation did not belong in her dream. Brushing it aside, she refocused on David. He was broad-shouldered…beautiful…his skin glowing in the sun…. He was tracing figure eights now over her shoulder. He smelled like pheromones and coconuts….

"Shake her harder, David. God forbid, she could be in a coma."

"I don't think it's a coma, Bubby."

In the dream, David's voice was rich and low, but he stopped licking and started jostling her shoulder. The dream Nina frowned and shimmied, hoping he'd go back to licking, but he kept on shaking her. Peeved, she scooped up a handful of sand and chucked it at her ill-behaved lover.

A deep, loud *Ooof!* finally woke Nina from her dream. She opened her eyes to see David, fully clothed and bent at the waist. He was not smiling. In fact, his face, mere inches from hers, was screwed into a very tight grimace.

"Nope. Not a coma," he announced, squeezing the words through gritted teeth. Slowly, he backed away from the couch and tried to stand.

"It's going to take more than potato plaster to fix that," commented Johanna, who was standing on the other side of the glass coffee table, next to Bubby, whose blue eyes were the widest Nina had ever seen them.

"I'll get you a nice castor oil pack, Mr. David. Don't you worry."

"Castor oil? That works?" Bubby's eyebrows jerked up. "I work at a senior center. You got anything for prostates?"

Johanna and Bubby adjourned to the kitchen while David attempted to straighten.

Nina sat up and rubbed her eyes. Everything seemed a bit vague and discombobulated at the moment. Tilting her head at David as he tried to take a deep breath, she asked, "What's wrong?"

With his hands on his hips, he looked at her like she was crazy. "What's wrong, Miss Baxter, is that since you were fired from Hanson's, *my* life has been in an uproar." Finally, he took the breath he'd been after. "I think you're fired again."

* * *

A half hour later, Nina poked her head around David's half-open bedroom door. "Knock, knock." He'd retreated to his bedroom—limping—shortly after he'd suggested that she might need to look for work again posthaste. "May I come in?"

David stood at his dresser, putting on his watch. He'd showered and changed into lightweight brown corduroys and a round-necked ivory sweater that emphasized the breadth of his shoulders. When he heard Nina's voice, he turned and narrowed his gaze.

"Are you armed?"

Standing half-behind the door, Nina shrugged. "I wasn't armed last time."

"True. All right, come in. But don't hurt me."

Nina, who had also changed out of the work clothes she'd put on earlier, took a few steps into the room. "This is for you." She held up the castor oil pack Johanna had thrust into her hands.

"I thought you said you weren't armed."

"This is supposed to help you feel less, um, however you feel. Johanna says it's an old family remedy."

Accepting the dubious first aid, he weighed it in his hand. "Old family remedy, huh?" Cocking a brow, he glanced at Nina. "Do you think Johanna's family gets kicked in the groin a lot?"

"Maybe by Johanna."

David grinned. "She can be a little strong-willed. Did she give you a hard time?"

"Not really." Nina slid her hands into the back pockets of the Levi's 501s she'd donned after her shower. "She and Bubby looked like they might rumble at first."

"They seem to be getting along well now."

Nina rolled her eyes. "Too well. After I deliver your castor oil, I'm supposed to head back to the kitchen for my cold cures."

He gestured to her expression. "And you are dreading this why?"

"You're holding a towel soaked with enough oil to fry Big Bird and you can ask me that?" David's easy laugh broke some of Nina's tension. "Bubby's cure is chicken soup," she said, "which would be all right except that she insists we eat the chicken neck. She thinks it prevents pneumonia." David winced, and she nodded. "I have no idea what Johanna uses to cure a cold, and I'm afraid to find out."

"Raw lamb."

"I could be in denial, but right now I'm telling myself I heard you wrong."

"You didn't. She keeps my freezer stocked with raw lamb all winter." He glanced to the door and lowered his voice. "Defrosts it in the microwave then grinds it into little meatballs. Nasty."

"I'm going to gag just thinking about it."

"Don't. If she hears you cough, you're a dead woman walking." Taking her wrist he pulled her farther into his bedroom then softly closed the door. Conspiratorially, he whispered, "You'll be safer in here."

Nina felt like a teenager, alone in a "guy's" bedroom when she shouldn't be. "I can't stay here, forever," she said, wondering if the statement sounded as flirtatious to his ears as it did to hers.

Apparently not because David seemed completely relaxed when he sat on the bed. "No, but you may be able to hide out long enough for Johanna to leave the kitchen. Once she's busy doing something else, I'll show you my disappearing meatball trick. Works like a charm."

He studied the towel Nina had brought him. "It's still hot." Looking up, he mused, "I wonder what effect castor oil is supposed to have on groin injuries?"

It would be humiliating to blush because he said the word *groin*. However, because David's crotch had recently figured so prominently in her fantasies, Nina found total composure difficult to maintain.

"How is it?" She pointed in the appropriate direction.

David looked down, then up again. A mischievous glint lit his eyes. "It's mighty fine."

"I meant your injury!"

He composed his features into an ingenuous mask. "So did I."

Did not. Nina knew this was probably the most opportune moment she would have to discover whether David was as attracted to her as she was to him. They were alone in his bedroom…having a conversation about his groin. A woman at ease with her own sexuality, a woman who had the sophistication and chutzpah to honor her own desires, would look him in the eye and say simply, *David, I like you. There's no reason we can't explore a physical relationship if you like me, too.*

That was so proactive, she felt empowered just thinking it. Unfortunately, she was an *un*sophisticated woman with limited chutzpah.

David's eyes had fine crinkles at the corners. As he gazed at her, she had the impression that he was in a very good mood. His king-size bed was roomy, but his height and the breadth of his shoulders suggested that a woman would not get lonely on the big mattress. She had nothing to lose, really, and perhaps a lot to gain by finding out how he felt.

"David," she said, trying to speak above the thunderous roar that rushed to her ears the moment she opened her mouth. She could feel her heart begin to sprint as if she'd run a mile in seven minutes. "David, Samantha mentioned that a few people in the office might have gotten the impression we're having an affair."

She watched him closely. His reaction would tell her a great deal. A man who was interested in a woman would maintain eye contact, smile suggestively and murmur something ambiguous, like, *Does that bother you?*

David bowed his head, pressed a thumb and forefinger to his brow bone and said, "My fault." Lowering his hand, he looked at Nina with patent regret. "My fault entirely."

Not a good sign. Nina felt her heart sink as he stood and walked toward her.

She looked up—way up—into his face as he put his hands on her shoulders. Regret sobered his expression.

"I mentioned that I'd hired you and that you were living with me. I thought it would be better for all of us if I put that fact on the table right away. I've got to host a business dinner sooner than I thought, and I didn't want the party to ignite speculation." His hands tightened on her shoulders. "I intended to defuse interest, not stir it. You have my word that I won't compromise your integrity in any way."

She felt his hands tighten once more and then release her. "On that note," he said, moving to the bedroom door and opening it, "hiding out in here probably wasn't a great idea." His smile returned, along with the wry tone. "If your grandmother or Johanna wanders this way, they'll have us married before the sun sets."

Stepping aside, he waited for her to exit the room ahead of him.

Defeated, she moved forward and caught a whiff of the clean, light cologne he used—or perhaps it was the pheromones she was starting to go nuts for. This wasn't right. Thirty-two, and she couldn't unearth the simple question *Are you attracted to me?* with both hands and a shovel.

Stopping directly beside her boss, she looked up and smiled at him a little weakly. Then she reached over, put a hand on the door and pushed it closed.

Chapter Eleven

The thing about bold moves, Nina realized, was that once you made one you had to follow it up with something equally bold. Otherwise, you wound up looking like a schlemiel.

So after she closed the bedroom door, she stood schlemiel-like while David gazed down at her in question.

"I'm not upset that people thought we were living in—" She stopped herself right before she said *sin*. How archaic was that?

Apparently she didn't stop herself soon enough. David's deep brown eyes widened. "Living in…?"

Wishing she'd bitten her tongue a sentence ago, she fumbled. "Living in… Dating."

David hooked one brow and deadpanned, "Living in dating."

"No, I mean, dating. Just dating. Never mind. I wasn't upset when Samantha told me what people thought." Because she wasn't used to telling fibs— even harmless fibs in the interest of seduction— Nina's mouth started working on the truth before her mind had a chance to orchestrate it. "Well, I was a little upset. I was pretty upset. It bothered me."

Humor suffused David's expression. Frustrated with herself, she socked him lightly on the shoulder. "What I mean is I wasn't angry with you. Samantha said you set the record straight right away."

"I did."

"Thank you."

"You're welcome."

Nina smiled. And silently said a word she'd once grounded Zach for using. Obviously her flirting skills had not made it into the new millennium; this seduction was too far gone to save.

As her eyes began to ache from sinus pressure, she acknowledged that this was a damned sorry time, anyway, to seduce a man who had dated the most beautiful women in Chicago. Her best efforts today had left her looking like the "before" photo for a NyQuil ad.

The problem with David, she decided, was that he was a chocolate-covered graham cracker. Nina never kept her favorite cookies in the house when she was dieting, because she understood that temptation trumped reason. David was the kind of cookie who should not be allowed in the house.

"Too bad we're single. If I had a boyfriend or you had a girlfriend, our living in the same house wouldn't be such an issue," she said, thinking it would help keep her head on straight, too.

David looked surprised. "If I had a girlfriend or you had a boyfriend, we wouldn't be living together at all, Miss Baxter."

He bent toward her, his lean-jawed face so close she could see flecks of gold in his eyes. "I don't know whom you've been dating," he purred in a liquid voice she'd never imagined her boss using, "but if you were my lover, you would not be sleeping in another man's home."

Nina felt herself sway as if hypnotized. "Oh."

Kiss me.

That was her only clear thought. It was just occurring to her that she might have to say it out loud when a bell rang. Multiple times.

As Nina tried to figure out whether the bell was a warning inside her head, David straightened and looked at the closed bedroom door. "Company," he murmured.

In the next moment, Nina heard Bubby and Johanna's voices, followed by a stampede of feet and the sound of her exuberant children. "The kids!" she moaned. She slapped a hand to her forehead. "Oh, no! I wanted to meet their bus."

Saying nothing, David nodded, reached over and opened the bedroom door.

Nina stepped into the hallway, expecting him to follow. When she heard the door click softly shut behind her and realized she was alone, she felt like she'd just ended a date. A bad one.

"You're absolutely certain you want to do this now?"

"Absolutely." Nina blew her nose and nodded vehemently. Her extraordinarily curly ponytail flopped heavily atop her head.

Five hours after she'd left his room this afternoon, David sat with Nina in his library. He peered intently at the calendar spread out on his desk, not because he needed to check dates, but because he didn't want to stare at her.

He'd barely been able to keep from picking her up and throwing first her and then himself onto the bed this afternoon.

Clearing his throat, he removed a pencil from a silver cup on his desk and stuck the tip in the electric sharpener. He had the ridiculous thought that the noise might mask the roar of his thoughts.

Nina Baxter was driving him crazy. He'd had to take several steadying breaths after she'd left his room. Then he'd dressed and joined the others as if nothing were out of the ordinary. He'd said hello to the kids, heard about their experience on a different school bus route, assured Johanna that her cure had worked wonders and had finally excused himself, saying he needed to head back to the office for a couple of hours. In reality he'd spent his time walking along the river, trying to clear his mind.

The instant he'd seen the insinuating tilt of his co-workers' raised eyebrows he had known that he would do nothing, *nothing,* to compromise Nina's reputation or her children's well-being. Didn't mean he'd decided he wasn't interested in something more than a boss-secretary relationship; it merely meant that he would force himself to decide exactly what that "something more" was before he took any action. The conclusion he'd come to while defending her integrity in the boardroom today was that he either had to marry Nina or fire her again so they could explore a relationship.

And then she'd stepped into his bedroom this afternoon. And had flirted. At least he was pretty sure she'd been flirting. He'd never seen it done quite that way before.

Accidentally allowing the electric sharpener to chew his pencil down to a mere shadow of its former self, David frowned, tossed it aside and plunged another helpless stick into the whirring blade.

"All right, let's get down to business," he said, removing the pencil before its demise and tapping the point on Friday of the current week. "You think you can pull together a small cocktail reception by this date?"

Nina leaned forward to view the day in question. She smelled like flowers and menthol, and instantly he had the image of the two of them ten years down the road, leaning over household accounts and discussing college funds.

He sat farther back in his chair. A woman's scent had affected him in the past, but never in that way. Blaming the vision of himself, domesticated in his fifties, on the menthol, he waited for Nina's response.

"Friday. That gives me four days," she said, nodding over the calendar. "Sure. Of course. Absolutely no problem." She swiped the tissue under her nose. "Tell me who's attending, how formal you want it and if you have anything special in mind, and I'll handle everything from there."

She sounded confident, even enthusiastic, but David didn't want to overtax her. His long-suffering secretary, who'd called him a workaholic slave driver for the past twenty years, would hit him with her hole punch if she could read his mind right now.

"Great," he said, in lieu of babying her. "The party is to welcome Shiguro Taka and his wife, and the objective is to convince Taka Enterprises that Hanson Media Group is still a major player. You'll have to do all the hiring necessary. George and Helen used to host the business parties." He frowned. "I suppose you can call Helen and ask for referrals if you want to."

"But you would rather not?" she guessed, studying his face.

David rubbed the shadow of stubble appearing on his chin. "Their parties were always very formal. Big and showy, like George." He smiled wryly at his new assistant. "Frankly, I've eaten enough beluga caviar to last me until the next ice age. I'm wondering how we could achieve a similar effect—enforcing the idea that the company is thriving again—without sacrificing…" David wasn't sure of the word he wanted.

"Warmth?" Nina suggested.

He nodded slowly. "Warmth. Yes. Hospitality."

"Something a little more old-fashioned and homey?" she ventured.

"Do you think old-fashioned, homey and warm can be impressive?"

Nina laughed. He thought the sound, husky and low, was distractingly sexy. "Obviously you've never been to a bar mitzvah."

For the next three days, Nina was too busy with decisions, plans and preparations to spend much time picturing David naked.

Well, she managed a couple of brief fantasies, but she was determined not to stray from her goal: to throw a party that Shiguro Taka would remember and that would make any and all suspicious minds realize that David had hired her because she was competent, creative and smart.

The first thing Nina did was check into caterers, but their ideas for a "warm and homey" soiree all sounded similar: mini hamburgers, hibachi cocktail dogs, custard cups of macaroni and cheese, individual meat loaves. Nina pictured tiny portions of mashed potatoes and gravy served alongside with eensy-weensy utensils. The image made her laugh, but the price of the all-American cocktail party did not. Making a mental note to go into catering if the business world completely dried up for her, Nina hung up with the last caterer and suddenly remembered what she'd said to David: *Obviously you've never been to a bar mitzvah.*

Why not?

She called Bubby. Together they planned the party and worked like fiends every minute that the kids were in school and David was at the office.

When they needed extra help in the kitchen, Nina called Janet Daitch, the grandmother approaching retirement age who had also been fired from Hanson's. And Bubby asked two of her friends from the senior center to bake challahs. All the women were thrilled to be cooking and baking "professionally."

Not only was Nina planning a very enjoyable cocktail party and giving good people a chance to earn a little extra cash, she was also saving David a truckload of money, which inspired her to add a new goal to her agenda: Show him and anyone else who cared to observe that one did not have to break the bank to have a good time. It was better to cut expenses than employees.

Each night when David came home, Nina would tell him only that the party plans were progressing nicely. She didn't want him to know that she and Bubby were preparing the food. She knew he'd balk, though she trusted that his resistance to the idea would stem from concern about her working too hard, not from lack of faith in her ability. That revelation evoked a sweet gratitude that made her all the more determined to plan a party he could be proud of.

For three days and three nights, Nina worked and planned and budgeted. When David arrived home to see her still fussing over her accounts ledger, he retired to his office. But he always emerged in time for popcorn and a movie with the kids.

On Thursday, with the plans and preparations looking good, Nina decided to do something about her own appearance. For years and years, she'd looked like exactly what she was: a single working mother on a budget. One who'd forgotten that even penny-pinching single mothers deserved a decent hairstyle.

Seeing Samantha again had sparked Nina's imagination. David expected her to be the hostess of this gathering; that called for something more than a skirt with a pattern that camouflaged jam stains and a hair claw to scrape her unruly curls into place. Samantha had curly hair, too, but she embraced the wildness. Her wardrobe was eclectic and creative and fun.

So, on Thursday when Nina called Samantha to formally confirm that she and Jack would be at the cocktail party, she stole an informal moment to ask the other woman about hair care.

Samantha did more than advise; she came over Friday on her lunch hour with hair products from Barneys in New York and showed Nina how to work with thick curly hair so that she looked more like Andie MacDowell than Roseanne Roseannadanna.

When Bubby and the other women Nina had hired to work in the kitchen that day noted the change in her appearance, they went to work on her wardrobe, promising to return that evening with items for her to try on.

David returned home after Nina had showered and experimented with the hair products Samantha had left. To her surprise and pleasure she was able to replicate the style Samantha had shown her earlier. Now for the first time in memory, her loose curls were soft and spiraling.

Because she was still waiting to see what the other women had chosen for her to wear, she was dressed in black warm-up pants with a white Maroon 5 T-shirt Zach had given her last Mother's Day.

"Hi," she said as she emerged from her room to find David walking down the hallway toward his office. He paused when he saw her, his expression plainly surprised. "Don't worry," she laughed, "I won't wear this to the cocktail party. I'm going to get dressed a little later."

"You look great."

She plucked at her T-shirt. "If this is 'great,' I definitely need to rethink my style."

David was dressed in his suit from work, his tie loosened, but not removed completely. He *did* look great, although a bit rough around the edges. His eyes were tired, his hair looked as if he'd been pushing his fingers through it, and he could use a shave. He still looked like John Corbett. On a good day. Not the kind of guy you'd kick out of bed for eating crackers.

Or for any other reason, Nina thought, immediately slapping a benign smile on her face. This was not the time to lust after the boss.

"We still have an hour and a half before the guests arrive," she ventured, changing the subject in her mind, "and half an hour before the crew shows up. So, I was wondering… It's Friday night, and the kids and I always celebrate Shabbat when we're home. If it's all right with you, I'd like to have a short service with them. Light the candles, say kiddush. Then they're spending the night with friends."

David looked bemused. "I'm not really sure what you're talking about, but sure. Go ahead." He smiled.

Nina smiled, too, and explained. "In observant Jewish families, we celebrate the end of the current week and the start of the coming week even when we're not in a synagogue. Especially when we're not in a synagogue. The Sabbath is a special day set aside for family and for reflection. Ideally," she added, since she'd moved on a Saturday and was working tonight. "Officially it begins at sundown on Friday and ends at sundown on Saturday. There's another service called havdalah that officially ends the Sabbath day."

David listened closely, but his expression was hard to read. Nina laughed. "Speaking of all things official, that officially ends my lecture on basic Judaism. Anyway, we'll be brief, and I'll make sure we don't disturb anything set up for tonight."

"I don't care what you disturb. Do you know your eyes get bluer when you talk about this?"

Nina didn't know about her eyes, but she felt her cheeks turn redder. "It's a passion for me. A way to connect with the past and the future. A way to bless the present."

"Do Zach and Izzy appreciate it the way you do?"

"They're beginning to. Izzy loves to light the candles. Plus there's really good bread and ultra-sweet wine involved."

David grinned. "Count me in. Are you starting right now?"

"Hmm?"

He loosened his tie and whipped it off his neck. "I'd like to join you, if I may. I can shower and change later if you want to get right to it."

Nina's eyes widened. "Oh!" A myriad of responding emotions left her speechless. "We can wait for you."

The anticipation she felt was surely sweeter than it should have been.

"Barukh ata Adonai Eloheinu…"

David didn't understand the Hebrew words and couldn't have repeated them if they'd been printed on a paper right in front of him. But understanding them didn't matter, not tonight. He understood that much right away.

"…melekh ha o-lam…."

The sounds and sights before him played on his heart…no, on something bigger, something that would never die… It played on his soul like his first glimpse of the ocean, the first sighting of an eagle.

Watching Nina and her daughter, their heads covered in lace, faces bathed in candlelight, eyes closed, lips parted to utter an ancient prayer as they held hands—it was a sight that stirred him more than he'd ever, ever have guessed.

The Friday-night candles were lit and the candle-lighting prayer sung by the women in a family, Nina had said, and David could see the wisdom in that tradition: No man would be able to think of work, of annoying traffic, of the bottom line while watching his wife and his daughter turn into angels right before his eyes.

If a man had a wife and a daughter.

David stood on the opposite side of the kitchen counter with Zach, watching and changing a little bit, though he wasn't sure how, with each small ritual of the service.

After the candle lighting, Zach, Izzy and Nina sang a happy song in Hebrew and English about greeting a Sabbath bride. They each listed one thing they had done well in the week past, one thing they were grateful for and one thing they wanted to do better in the week ahead. When Nina looked at David to see if he wanted to contribute anything to that part of the proceedings, he was so filled with emotion, so unsure what he was feeling exactly that he shook his head slightly, something he regretted when her list included gratitude for the work she'd been given and the hospitality she and her children had been shown.

Nina then had Zach bring out a handmade box with Hebrew lettering. She thanked God that her family had "plenty," and that they were able to give daily to others, at which point she, Zach and Izzy all reached into their pockets to place money inside the box. Nina placed dollar bills; her kids dropped in change.

"There are kids in Chicago who have to sleep on the street. That's me and Zach's *Tzedakah* project," Izzy said.

"*Tzedakah* is a form of charity," Nina clarified. "But really it's about remembering that we're all connected, all responsible for each other in some way, so when one person is hurting, we have to notice and care. Izzy and Zach drop in change each day and when they have ten dollars, they give it to a women-and-children's shelter. *Tzedakah* is a daily practice, but it's especially powerful on the Sabbath. It's part of repairing the world."

David dropped in a ten, but watching two preteen kids dig into their pockets and say a prayer, asking God to make the money do good work, left him with a vague unease. Hanson's grand donations and lavish charity events seemed small, almost embarrassing by comparison.

In David's family, no one had ever prayed at home. The family had trekked to church on Christmas and Easter, but once they'd left the building, prayer was forgotten in favor of more business. Always the business. David remembered thinking that for the Hansons, going to church was like visiting an elderly relative: You didn't want to go, the cookies were good, you couldn't wait to leave. He wished now that his parents had talked to him about the meaning behind the moments. He wished they'd talked more, period. And touched.

David emerged from his uncomfortable musing when Zach moved to stand next to his mother and Izzy. Nina put a hand on each of her children's heads, thanked God for "blessing me with these beautiful people," and asked Him to remind Izzy daily that she was strong, loving and kind and to remind Zach that he was compassionate, wise and noble.

David could have sworn that the kids grew taller in that moment beneath the cap of her hand. He had a sudden, disturbing memory of himself seated between his parents in church on an Easter Sunday. His father had opened the paper program and was scribbling office memos over the words to "Amazing Grace." His mother was staring straight ahead, a bland smile on her face, her mind obviously elsewhere. But the parents in the pew ahead had their arms around their kids and when it was time to stand and sing, each parent held a hymnal with one hand and put a free arm around the nearest child. David had inched his own hymnal closer to his mother so she could sing with him, but she hadn't noticed.

It was no wonder he found this moment of candlelight, song and family to be almost painfully full of grace.

He began thinking he might excuse himself, get ready for the party, when Zach announced, "Time for *hamotzi!*"

The boy placed his hands on a plate covered by an attractive embroidered cloth. Izzy and Nina each touched one of Zach's shoulders while Zach said a prayer, again in Hebrew. His mother and sister joined him on "Amen!" and the cloth was removed to reveal a fragrant golden-brown loaf of bread that was braided to resemble a fat blond pigtail.

A bread knife was eschewed in favor of breaking the bread by hand. The inside of the loaf was pale butter-yellow, soft and sweet-smelling, and the rustic appearance of the broken hunk seemed in keeping with the evening's theme of honoring the past while ushering in the future.

The big surprise came when Nina broke off two small bites of bread and placed one each in her children's mouths. Then Zach and Izzy broke off two pieces and took turns putting those in Nina's mouth.

While Nina chewed, Izzy spun around to look at David. "Now you!" she said. She tugged on her mother's shirt. "Someone has to feed David."

Nina raised a brow, silently asking if he was willing. "We feed each other the challah." She raised the larger hunk still in her hand. "It's symbolic."

Something happened in his stomach, some gnawing yearning that was stronger than hunger. He looked at her, springing hair glowing in the candlelight, face and eyes shining from the inside out.

Moving toward the threesome, but unable to take his eyes off Nina, he nodded. *Yes. Feed me.*

Under the watchful eyes of her two children, Nina broke off a piece of the bread and lifted it to David's mouth. From David's perspective, the scene seemed to play out in slow motion.

He opened his mouth and felt the brush of her cool fingers against his lower lip as she fed him the bite of challah. He felt his heart pound, felt the sweet, yeasty taste burst on his tongue. Bread had never been this good.

She began to step away, but David stopped her by reaching for the challah still in her hand. Locking his gaze with hers, he raised the bread to her mouth and felt the same heart-pounding anticipation, the same burst of sweetness as he fed her.

The candle flames danced light around the room and illuminated the pinkness of Nina's cheeks.

"Well, that's how our family celebrates Shabbat," she said breathily, a puff of sweet, self-conscious laughter trailing the words. "Now you know what you've been missing."

"Now I know," he murmured.

But David had an inkling—no, he was certain—that he'd only just begun to discover what he'd been missing.

Chapter Twelve

"Shiguro Taka just told his wife to get the recipe for the brisket." Samantha waylaid Nina and pulled her into the hallway for a brief conversation. "You're brilliant. Everyone's so into the food they're actually relaxed and chatting like normal people at a party instead of suits with martinis in their hands."

Nina breathed a sigh of relief. Actually it may have been her first full breath since David had put the bread in her mouth.

Samantha looked smashing. Confident and unique as always in a dress made from some filmy material that looked like a watercolor painting. Coming from her, the thumbs-up gave Nina a welcome shot in the arm. She hadn't had time to trade more than a word or two with David since the first guests had arrived. She didn't know how he felt about her decidedly Yiddish soiree.

Carved brisket, miniature potato kugels, mini bagels and lox, tiny hot pastrami sandwiches on mini rounds of rye, and chopped liver spiked with port (which several people had deemed the finest "pâté" they had ever eaten)—the food was definitely a hit, devoured with the kind of gusto that would make any Jewish mama kvell with joy.

Looking over Samantha's shoulder, she watched the twenty or so guests laugh and mingle with plates in their hands.

The room glowed, lit by candles and lamps with amber bulbs. Music was provided by the grandson of one of Bubby's friends at the senior center, who sang in low tones and accompanied himself on the guitar.

"Do you think David is happy with the evening?" Nina heard the puppy-dog eager-to-please-ness in her own voice. She may as well have wagged her tail and peed on the floor. Smoothing the pale blue silk skirt she'd been lent for the evening, she looked away as if the answer didn't mean all that much and hoped Samantha had missed the too-vulnerable tone.

"David's usually a little stiff at these things." The other woman pursed her lips. "I've asked Jack if the Hansons have a genetic mutation I ought to know about, something that makes them sound like European royalty in the 1940s. Have you noticed that?"

Nina nodded. "I told David he sometimes sounds like Rex Harrison."

Samantha laughed. "Jack says his brothers got all the wild and crazy genes. He got an extra dose of responsibility."

"Does that bother him?"

"I think so." Raising a white-chocolate martini to her lips, Samantha let the drink linger on her tongue then giggled. "At least, it bothered him enough to prove to me he can be wild and crazy when it counts."

When Nina's eyes widened at the revelation, Samantha laughed again and patted her shoulder. "Anyway, I've noticed that Jack and David get more formal when there are a lot of people around or when they're nervous."

"You think David's nervous?"

Samantha shook her head. "I think David looks more relaxed tonight than I've seen him at any business function. You've done a great job. Don't worry."

Nina nodded and Samantha trailed off in search of Jack. Nina did worry, though. She knew she'd gone out on a limb tonight. Everything from the food to the decorations to the people who were serving had been organized on a self-imposed budget with Nina's own agenda in mind.

As yet unbeknownst to David, both servers were recently "released" Hanson employees. They had experience in food service, and it had seemed…well, just plain *wrong* to use a catering service when Nina knew that Janet and Gillian were still looking for jobs. They'd been glad to get her call and though they hadn't been happy to be fired, neither did they appear to hold a grudge against anyone at Hanson. Nina was sure they would conduct themselves professionally, but she wished she'd thought to pull David aside and warn him.

Stretching on tiptoe, she looked for him among the milling guests. Before she found him, however, she spotted Gillian.

Circulating with a tray of mini bagels and lox, Gillian had been waylaid by Les Deland, a Hanson exec, who was pointing at her and squinting. Gillian had worked in accounts payable and claimed she'd never mingled much with the Hanson execs or board of directors, but Les looked like he was trying to place her or had already recognized her. More troubling was Gillian's response: Glancing nervously around the room, she appeared to be looking for Nina.

Foreboding crept fingerlike up Nina's spine. What if one or more of the guests really did take exception to her choice in hiring? What if they thought that populating a Hanson PR party with recently laid-off employees was a bad idea? They would blame David.

Heading immediately for the plate-glass windows where Gillian and Les Deland stood, Nina began to entertain a host of worries, all of which ended with

David losing the trust of his colleagues because of her. Why had she tried to impose her values on his party without even checking with him?

When she reached the duo, she heard Les Deland, a portly gentleman with a generally jovial disposition and prematurely receding hairline say to Gillian, "Aw, come on, meet me after the party. We can get sushi. There's a place in my neighborhood that stays open till two."

"Oh, there's my boss!" Gillian said, her voice sounding worried, but her eyes wide with relief as Nina stopped beside them. "I'd better take this tray around."

Les didn't catch the relief part. He patted Gillian's arm. "Don't worry. I've got some pull here." He winked. To Nina, he said, "I hope you won't chastise this lovely young woman for sharing a few words with me. I fell in love with her bagels and lox before I fell for her. Maybe you can convince her to have dinner with me?"

Now that she was close enough to look into his eyes, it seemed to Nina that Les Deland had ingested more bourbon than bagel this evening. Before she could respond to his soggy request, a broad hand slapped Les on the back. "Good to see you enjoying yourself."

David's warm voice betrayed not a hint of disapproval.

"I'm having a terrific time," Les confirmed, raising a glass that contained nothing but ice. "Best party I've been to all year."

"Good. That's what we like to hear. Where's your lovely wife?" David glanced around. "Is she here?"

Les's puffy cheeks reddened. Looking down at his glass, he mumbled something. The only words Nina caught were *visiting* and *sister*.

"Tell her we missed her," David said, still betraying not a hint of censure, though Nina thought that someone who knew him well would surely notice the steel behind the smile. "The Takas were just asking me about tickets to the Oprah Winfrey show," he said, his hand still on Les's shoulder. "Mrs. Taka would like to go. Why don't you look into that?"

While Les nodded, David told Gillian he was sure Mr. and Mrs. Taka would love to try the lox and bagels if they hadn't already, which gave Gillian the chance to slip away.

Nina felt a whoosh of relief now that the incident was over, until David requested, "May I have a word with you, Miss Baxter?" She couldn't help but notice that the conviviality in his expression had grown a bit…set.

Uh-oh.

"Certainly, Mr. Hanson," she answered pleasantly, as businesslike as she could be, but that foreboding tingle was back.

"We can speak in my office," he said and led the way.

David walked easily around the pockets of party guests, all dressed in designer clothing and coiffed to studied perfection. He fit right in among them. On the way to his office, he smiled, nodded and traded a word or two here and there, all without actually stopping. The glances from other men were always courteous, sometimes deferential. From the women, he received open admiration and, twice, lingering looks that were frankly flirtatious. David never broke stride. He was obviously a man who had spent his career cultivating respect, and he'd come to take it for granted.

His brother's dishonesty and the ensuing problems at the company must have been an open sore to a man like David. He intended to use this and subsequent parties to heal the wounds. He'd made that clear to Nina. Which once again called into question her decision to hire ousted Hanson employees without even running it by him first. She hoped he would consider the fact that his guests appeared to be enjoying themselves, but her feet began to drag heavily as she trailed behind him. Something in the way he'd looked at Gillian told her that the catering staff would indeed be the topic of their conversation.

By the time she stood in the former library, she'd rehearsed, *We'll leave in the morning,* a dozen times.

"Will you close the door, please?" David spoke

while glancing at some papers on his desk. He didn't even make eye contact with her.

When the latch clicked, David looked up, bland and businesslike. "Have a seat. This won't take long."

"If it won't take long, I think I'll stand."

"Have a seat."

"Don't mind if I do."

She perched on the edge of a designer chair, and waited.

David leaned a hip on his desk, loosely clasped hands resting on one thigh. "I went to the kitchen for an aspirin," he said. "Your grandmother certainly is busy in there."

Nina got the point. She hadn't mentioned yet that she and Bubby had made all the food themselves. She'd decided to wait until after he realized how delicious it was.

"I was glad to see she had help," David continued, his tone deceptively conversational. "Jog my memory. I'm great with faces, but not as good with names. Who is the woman slicing the pastrami?"

"Janet Daitch."

"Right. And I recognize her because she works at Hanson Media Group. Correct?"

"*Worked* at Hanson Media Group."

David's expression did change then, growing somber, tighter. "The laid-off grandmother who was looking forward to retirement." He remembered what she'd told him the day she'd lectured him about firing employees and eating at restaurants with Michelin stars.

"What about the woman Les was bothering?" he asked.

"Gillian." Nina sighed. In for a penny. "Gillian Roesch. Accounts payable."

"Laid off?"

"With the first wave of cutbacks. She has three kids under five. And waitressing experience," Nina said in her own defense.

David's expression remained impassive. "What about the other server? Short dark hair."

"Amanda Barker. She'd only been at Hanson a couple of weeks before the layoffs," Nina said hopefully, as if that would make her decision to hire much more palatable. "And she really prefers waitressing."

He nodded, slowly and without ever taking his eyes off her. Guilt crept along the edges of Nina's mind. She'd wanted to "teach" David and his fellow execs about budgeting and loyalty to employees, but she hadn't shown much loyalty to him. Ever since she'd thrown things at him he had done nothing but attempt to make amends for her job loss. He had tried to improve her circumstances.

She had complicated his.

"If I was half as smart as I think I am, I'd fire you."

Nausea and regret rose in Nina's throat. Under the circumstances she couldn't blame him, but the sense of loss she felt swelled like a wave she needed to jump.

He stood away from the desk, which made him tower over her. "You're wasted here. I don't know what I was thinking. I ought to hire you to assist with in-house public relations. In fact, the more I think about it, the better firing you as my personal assistant sounds."

Perched on the chair while he hovered above her, Nina felt her mind swirl with indecision. Should she begin apologizing now? Walk away with dignity? Beg for her job so her children could eat next week?

She pushed to her feet, willing, at least, to ask that he please allow the other women to finish the night's work.

David's expression was unreadable, his handsome face a construction of chiseled angles and clean curves.

"Do you think I should fire you?" His voice was softer now. Subtle. His warm baritone melded the words together like a song, making her fear subside. Milk-chocolate eyes gazed at her like he was a layer of frosting and she was the cake.

What was the question?

"Think about it, Nina. If you weren't my personal assistant, it wouldn't be quite so wrong to do this."

He'd anticipated her resisting. He'd half expected himself to stop before he actually kissed her.

But when David put his hands on Nina's arms and drew her toward him, lowered his head…closer… closer…closer…neither of those two things happened. He didn't stop and she didn't pull away.

There was a world of surprise and awe in that
kiss. For David, at least. He couldn't tell what Nina
was feeling. At first it was difficult to focus on her
response because he was too involved in the taste of
her and in resisting the pull to delve his fingers into
the masses of thick looping curls. *Go slow, go slow*
was the chant that thrummed through his brain, but
desire clashed against it like a competing cymbal.

He remembered that he was kissing someone who
hadn't asked to be kissed, who hadn't indicated in
any way that she wanted to make their relationship
physical, so he worked his mouth more slowly over
hers, testing and questioning until he knew they were
on the same page.

More or less the same page. What David sensed
from Nina was that she was willing; he, on the other
hand, wanted to end the party now, clear out the
house and carry her to his bedroom. And he didn't
want to come out for at least twenty-four hours.

Through his suit jacket, he felt her hands curl
around his triceps. He wanted to rip off the jacket and
growl, "Touch me!" To avoid frightening either her
or the guests in the other room, however, he contented himself by releasing her arms to slide his
hands up toward her collarbone.

She was wearing a silky pale blue top with a round
neck that gave him easy access to the delicate,
creamy skin, dusted with freckles so small they
looked like glitter. He merely pictured those freck-

les now as he trailed the pads of his fingers over the silky skin, eyes closed as she shivered and he deepened the kiss. He gave himself another minute before he had to pull away or lock the damned door and take her now on the Berber carpet.

He ran a hand to the back of her neck, slipped his tongue past her open lips and felt himself grow harder than granite as she opened her mouth.

If he'd been twenty years younger he wouldn't have considered stopping. Not when her tongue met his, not when he felt her fingers tighten as if she had to cling to his arms to keep from falling down.

Yes. This was what he wanted. This woman. At this time in his life. *Bring your baggage, bring it all, Nina Baxter. And let me touch you, let me inside, because I've never wanted to be anyplace more.*

He slipped a knee between her legs, moved his hands down her back to hold her when she swayed. The fire he was playing with consumed her, too.

To hell with stopping. All they had to do was figure out how to get out of here so he could take her to a hotel room. Jack could close the damned party.

David's brain tried to work, but with most of his blood rushing downward, it wasn't easy. He decided to clue Nina in on what he was thinking and gently, with great difficulty, pushed her away.

Lust made his heart pound, which in turn roughened the edges of his voice. "Listen—"

"David, the Takas are leaving, and I— Oh. Sorry! Oh."

Nina jumped when she heard Jack's voice. Swiveling in David's arms, she looked at the door and saw what he did: Jack *and* Samantha stood on the threshold, Jack looking flummoxed, Samantha surprised and trying not to grin. David felt Nina's muscles turn rigid, though they'd been as soft as cooked noodles only a moment before.

David, the soul of patience if he said so himself, wanted to wring his nephew's neck. "Do you knock?"

"I did, actually. Twice." For the first time in ages, sheepish Jack looked more like David's nephew than Hanson's CEO.

The truth was Jack could have knocked a dozen times, and David wouldn't have heard him. Unfortunately he was in no mood to be reasonable. "Well, did you hear me say, 'Come in'?"

"No, that's true. But I, uh…" Jack looked at Samantha. "Why did I open the door?"

Rubbing her fiancé's shoulder, Samantha prompted, "Because we're leaving, and we want to say goodbye like polite guests." She addressed David. "Also Shiguro is looking for you."

"Right." Jack nodded, taking Samantha's hand. "The Takas want to say goodbye and thank you. Les said he saw you heading this way, so I thought I'd…" He frowned at his uncle's still unpleasant expression. Calmly, he turned toward his bride-to-be. "I think we're done here."

Samantha smiled. "Almost. Great party," she said to both David and Nina. "Listen, don't bother to answer now, but will you consider hosting our bridal shower? I want Bubby to cater. I'm mad about the liver or pâté or whatever you want to call it. Think it over." Mischief infused her falsely innocent expression. As the door closed behind her and Jack, she leaned around for one more smile and a huge thumbs-up.

"Subtle, isn't she?" David murmured when the door had clicked. "Hard to believe we're going to be related."

Nina took a step away and shivered. She didn't look at him as she smoothed the top and skirt he'd only just begun to muss.

"Don't even think about walking out of here," he said, drawing a glance of surprise.

"The Takas are looking for you," she reminded him. "You don't want to hide from your guests of honor." Her voice was a bit shaky, not nearly as matter-of-fact as she wanted it to sound. David took great comfort in that.

Reaching for her arm, he drew her close and held her, letting his fingers play in the tumbled cloud of curls the way he'd wanted to all evening. He didn't try to kiss her again; that would have been counterproductive.

"I'm not forgetting the Takas," he assured, weaving a thick curl around his finger while his other hand stroked her back. She shivered again. "But I'm not leaving this room until I can make a G-rated appearance."

Nina pulled back to look at him quizzically. Then her expression cleared, and, to his great delight, a smile played across her rosebud lips when she realized that although he had put the brakes on their kissing session, his body was still very much in drive.

Chapter Thirteen

Nina was rinsing the champagne flutes and matching china plates she'd rented for the evening when David entered the kitchen. It was after 11:00.

The condo was still redolent with aromas from the food they'd served all evening. Tangible reminders of the savory brisket and hot pastrami mingled with the subtle, lingering scents of two-hundred-dollar-an-ounce perfumes.

Mostly what Nina would recall from this evening, however, was the surprise of David's kiss and the way it had excavated an aching awareness of her own loneliness. For years she had buried her personal needs, denied having any that couldn't be postponed indefinitely.

She'd believed she could live for her children, her responsibilities and then remember herself…someday.

It appeared that today was the day.

Every cell of her being had come awake with David's touch. His kisses made her remember why the first flowers of spring were so welcome after a long bare winter. She didn't know if he'd want to pick up where they'd left off when Jack had interrupted, or if he was thinking, *Whew, that was a close call*. But she knew she'd cry in bed tonight if she had to sleep alone.

She would have sex with him if he asked.

The knowledge was exhilarating. Terrifying. Like an extreme sport.

He said nothing as he crossed the kitchen to stand beside her. They were alone now in the condo, guests gone and her children at their friends' house until tomorrow. David stood so close she could smell his skin—warm and musky with the memory of his aftershave. Nina felt her heart wobble as if each beat took all her body's effort. Beneath the running water, her hands trembled around.

David reached for the faucet and turned off the water. Taking the glass from her slippery hands, he set it aside, picked up a dish towel lying over the lip of the sink and wiped her fingers…gently, thoroughly…one by one.

When her hands were dry, he ditched the towel and drew her toward him until their torsos touched… and then their hips…the tops of their thighs…. Fire burned.

David released her hands after he'd guided them around his waist. He'd discarded his coat, and Nina felt the solidness, the strength and power in his body.

He plowed fingers through her hair, tilted her face and kissed her with all the desire and none of the restraint he'd grappled for earlier in the evening.

Nina gave herself up to the kiss. Her hands refused to stay primly around his waist. She wanted to touch his back, his shoulders, his neck where it sloped into collar and chest. She cupped a palm around his jaw and felt it move when his tongue slipped between her lips. Every time she thought of a new place to touch, she followed the desire with action. David did the same.

Two minutes into the kiss, it seemed as if they were merely seconds away from slipping to the kitchen floor to make love. The urgency of his need was evident in the sudden roughness of his hands, the ragged breathing, the hardness that pressed against her pelvis. Nina was more than willing to make love where they stood, without breaking the moment, without thinking or speaking. No space between desire and consummation.

In the end, they moved out of the kitchen and down the hall. David's room was the unspoken destination, though how they got there she couldn't remember later. Clothes were pushed and pulled, hiked up and down, but not removed completely. They fell onto the king-size bed, and the only pause Nina noticed was the one during which he reached into a drawer for a condom, and she tugged off her pantyhose. After that, it was all hungry mouths and even hungrier hands.

He reached for her, made sure she was ready, but words dissolved into groans and groans to gasps. There was no time for teasing, and no patience for it. Like teenagers who hadn't any idea how to wait, or clandestine lovers who couldn't afford to, they tore remaining barriers out of their way. David made quick work of her underwear. Then, breathing like a thoroughbred nearing the end of a race, he opened her body to his and drove inside.

Nina moaned at the pleasure and the pain of re-awakening. David pushed deeper, gave and took, and they rocked together until they could no longer breathe.

David knew true satisfaction for perhaps the first time in his life.

Standing at the window of his downtown office, he looked at the street below, but saw only Nina.

For sixteen hours he'd had her all to himself. They'd slept for part of that time, but she'd been in his dreams, too, and when he'd awakened, he'd opened his eyes to her beautiful face…had felt her touching him.

The first time they'd made love, he'd been almost ashamed of his need, of the urgency that hadn't allowed him even to disrobe fully. But Nina's need had matched his. And he'd made it up to her, later that night and most of the next day.

Gazing out the spotless window, he grinned, finally managing to notice the sky and wondering if Chicago was always this cloudless and sunny in early May.

Making love to Nina had scrubbed away a good quarter century of dusty cynicism.

He'd spent Sunday showing the Takas around Chicago. Even though Nina had begged off to take Izzy and Zach to a music recital, David had thought Chicago never looked better, more interesting, more clean.

That night they'd all been together—David, Nina and the kids—and though he'd spent a good part of the evening wondering whether he and Nina would find a way to make love with two preteens in the house (they hadn't), he'd enjoyed that Sunday night at home more than any in memory.

Now it was eleven-thirty Monday morning, almost lunchtime. David had phoned home twice and had gotten the answering machine. He had no lunch meetings; going home to see Nina, to talk, to make love seemed like a much better plan than eating over his desk.

His secretary buzzed just as he was reaching for the phone.

"Mrs. Hanson is here to see you," she said.

It took a moment for him to realize whom Judy meant. "Helen?"

"She'd like to know if you have a few minutes before your next meeting."

Judy knew he didn't have another meeting until three that afternoon. She was giving him an out he'd love to take, but Helen, his sister-in-law, had never asked to see him at work before. Hoping it wouldn't take long, he responded, "Send her in."

The door opened. Helen entered as she'd entered every room since the first time he'd met her: She swept in; she glided. Blond, tall and as perfectly groomed as a Nieman Marcus mannequin, George's widow was as beautiful today as she'd been when George had first introduced her to David.

There was something different today, though. Something slightly off.

"I'm sorry I came over without calling first." She apologized before saying hello. "George hated it when I did that."

"How are you, Helen?" The perfunctory question emerged as just that: a polite rejoinder. It occurred to David almost immediately as he noted the unusual puffiness around Helen's eyes that if he *really* cared how his sister-in-law was faring, he'd have visited her at least once or twice since George had died. He felt a stab of guilt, though duller probably than it should have been.

She aimed her green eyes slightly to David's left as she replied, "Fine. May I sit down?"

He came around the desk, pulled out a chair Helen

had ordered upholstered in Thai silk the year she'd redecorated the offices.

Sitting behind his desk seemed too businesslike, so David hovered at its edge and waited for Helen to speak. He felt his brows pulling together by the time she formed her words.

"The reading of George's will is coming up," she began, her voice as unusually tentative as her gaze. "We haven't discussed George—you and I—since the funeral. I thought…"

In the uncertain pause, David wondered what, precisely, she wanted to discuss. Given the information that had come to light after George's death, affectionate reminiscence seemed unlikely. Even the eulogy David had delivered at the funeral had focused on George's exuberant personality, his business acumen, his commitment to excellence, but had neatly skirted personal details. George Hanson's death had brought one fact above others into bald relief: David hadn't known his brother.

It had never occurred to him, for instance, that George had kept a double set of books for the business, or that George had been so afraid of failure that he'd been willing to lie to his family and business associates for years.

"I'm not sure what to talk about," David began, deciding there had been enough courtesy. If Helen wanted to take a trip down memory lane, she'd have to find another travel companion; he couldn't do it, not yet. "If nothing else, these past months have proved to me that I didn't know my brother, Helen. I'd like to offer you some comfort…something…. I'm not sure—"

"I didn't know him, either!" Helen blurted, her green eyes large and worn from crying as she looked directly at David for the first time today. "That's why I'm here."

She dug into an ivory leather handbag the identical shade as her dress. David noticed then that the blond hair she'd pulled into a low coil at the nape of her neck was straight and tight, not big and curled, as she'd worn it for years. When she pulled out a large plain envelope, he saw, too, that she'd removed the gemstones that had previously decorated her long fingers.

She held the letter up, looking at David with unblinking pain. "George left me this. I found it a few days ago. He wrote it right before he died, apparently. As if he had a premonition."

She stopped speaking, but David's curiosity was peaked. He reached for the envelope.

As if his fingers were licks of fire, she snatched the letter to her bosom, away from his grasp. "It's written to me. It's…private."

"Then why are you—"

"I don't know!" Helen, truly agitated now, rose and paced the office. "I shouldn't have come. I shouldn't have, but I want to know if George ever said anything

to you…about me." She halted and looked at David
again. When her lips trembled, she set her jaw with
the determination of a fighter climbing into the ring.
"Did he tell you why he married me?"

Oh, hell. Apparently there were more surprises
from George. David wasn't sure he wanted to hear
this. Correction: He was damned sure he didn't. But
Helen was genuinely upset and clearly intent on answers, not platitudes.

"George didn't talk to me about personal issues,
Helen." He decided to start with broad truths and
work his way to specifics. "He always seemed proud
of you. Glad you were his wife—"

"Glad to show me off," she interrupted bitterly, her
eyes sparking now with more fire than he'd ever
credited her. "Did he ever use the word *love?* As in,
'Look at the little lady. Ain't she somethin'? I sure
do love her.'" Her lips pursed and she shook her
head. "No, I guess not."

Raising the letter, she looked at it as if she couldn't
decide whether to rip it to shreds or read it again. "He
apologizes in here." She spoke with her eyes on the
envelope, and with each word her tone flattened,
sounding more resigned. "He's sorry he wasn't able
to give me what I needed. Sorry he didn't have the
'emotion' I wanted." Her gaze rose. "He says he sus-
pects I'm smarter than he gave me credit for."

David was stunned. Even in the face of Helen's
palpable pain, he found himself amazed chiefly that

his brother had, after all, noticed other people's needs. That he'd felt some remorse.

He also realized the letter's less overt implication: George must have sensed that he was ill. Perhaps he'd felt some culpability for the mess he was about to bequeath his family.

Helen took a shuddering breath. When she looked at David, she was still full of emotion, but visibly calmer.

"Damned right I'm smarter than he gave me credit for," she said, admirably more resolute than angry. "Obviously not smart to accept the truth a long time ago—I was George's trophy wife. The second wife usually is, isn't she?" Her lips curled with eloquent irony. "But we trophy wives get older, too, and if we're lucky we grow up. Well, I'm smart enough to realize that my stepsons share their father's flaws. They don't know how to act like family, and they underestimate their stepmother."

She tucked the letter into her purse. "You've always been cordial to me, David. Cordial and, I think, honest. So I'm going to be honest with you. I realize that the Hanson men expect me to take my diamonds and my big house and pretend my involvement in this family is over. But it isn't. Not by a long shot. For better or worse George Hanson made me a stepmother and a shareholding member of Hanson Media Group. I intend to follow through on both responsibilities."

David didn't know exactly what she meant by that and wondered if Hanson Media Group or the Hanson family could survive too many more surprises.

He gestured to the abandoned chair. "Helen, why don't you sit down? It appears we have more to discuss." He reached for his phone. "I'll have some coffee brought in, and we can—"

"Do I sound like I need caffeine?" She managed to laugh. "No, David, that's enough for today." She looked at her watch. "I barged in. We'll talk more another day—when we both have more time, and I'm a little calmer." She offered a self-aware smile through her tears. "May I ask you not to mention this to the boys? Though I'm sure it would brighten their day to know their father cared for me about as little as they do."

The boys. George's sons, who had never been on fabulous terms with their young stepmama.

David frowned, but nodded, because despite her being distraught, today he'd witnessed in Helen a steely strength he'd never before attributed to her. And she was right about one thing: The Hansons didn't know how to be a family. If she thought she could straighten them out, why not give her a crack at it?

"I won't say anything until I hear from you again, Helen," he said. "But I hope that will be soon."

The smile she sent him was grateful. "It will be."

On high, thin heels, she walked out, and David felt suddenly exhausted. Running a hand through his hair, he decided he'd rather not know all that was in that letter. Shoving his restless hands in his pockets, he stalked to the window, but this time he saw nothing at all.

Good God, when he exited this world, would he be like his brother? Would he leave behind the same uncertainty, the doubt and division George had left?

Two of his sons couldn't even be bothered to show up for the reading of the damned will.

"You blew it, George. You had the people present and accounted for, but you didn't know how to turn them into a family."

That seemed to be a problem in the Hanson DNA.

David blinked, tried to focus his eyes, but instead of the Chicago skyline he saw Nina…Zach…Izzy… even Bubby.

The people. Present and accounted for.

The need to see Nina *now* welled inside him like lava looking for the top of the volcano.

He didn't want to sneak around, trying to have sex when no one was looking. He didn't want to be the lover who lurked in the shadows of her life.

David wasn't even certain what he was going to say to Nina when he got home. He wasn't sure she'd be there. Neither of those circumstances stopped him from picking up the phone and telling his secretary to reschedule his 3:00 p.m. meeting, then grabbing the jacket off the back of his chair and sprinting through the office until he reached the elevators.

He stepped onto the car with his heart hammering so hard he may as well have been walking up twenty flights of stairs, not taking the elevator down. Watching the numbers above the doors flash in decreasing double digits, he knew only one thing with absolute certainty.

Building a family was harder than building a business. And a whole helluva lot more exciting. Nina, her children and her bubby were the fulfillment he'd been looking for all his life.

Chapter Fourteen

From the moment she'd awakened Monday morning, Nina had sensed the day was going to be atypical. Usually ready to leap into her week, today she'd gotten in the shower and forgotten to wash her hair. Then she'd scorched the eggs she'd intended to give her kids for breakfast and had substituted a quick bowl of raisin bran with organic soy milk instead. Zach had said the soy milk tasted like "feet," but the new doctor had strictly prohibited dairy products until Zach's asthma was under control.

"I'll buy rice milk today," she'd promised her son, but he'd left for school grumpy and talking about child abuse.

Things hadn't gone much better with Izzy. Over the weekend, Isabella had announced her interest in becoming a vegetarian. Nina had thought her daughter would wade slowly into this new venture—if at all—and hadn't thought twice about making her daughter's beloved tuna sandwich with relish and olives on a kaiser roll for lunch. Izzy said she couldn't possibly eat anything that had had a mother, which eliminated the option of the school cafeteria's hamburger day. To insure that her children ingested something more than chips and soda, Nina had sent them to school then made a new lunch for Izzy, and a dairy-free, sugar-free, wheat-free snack for Zach. She drove to the school to deliver the parcels, and had just returned to the condo. It was 12:15, she hadn't had her own breakfast yet, and her shining face was a makeup-free zone.

She was finally sitting down to a bowl of oatmeal and the *Chicago Sun-Times* when David came through the front door.

A wide smile split her face. Probably had oatmeal between her teeth, but what the hell. She rose from the kitchen counter, crossed to him and moved easily into large, strong arms that promptly wrapped around her.

He rested his face in her hair. "Exactly the greeting I hoped for," he murmured. "Right down to the toes."

"Beg your pardon?"

Without moving to look at the digits in question, he said, "Your feet are bare. I noticed when I walked in. I like your bare feet, very uniform toes."

"Hmm." Nina snuggled more deeply into his embrace. There was definitely something to be said for a man's bulkier muscles; she felt locked in a warm, safe place. If they'd been dating awhile she might have told him all about her crappy morning and looked for a consoling smooch. Under the circumstance, she contented herself with the hug.

"Sit down," he said, giving her an affectionate pat on the rump. "Finish your…" He looked in the bowl and raised a brow. "Breakfast?"

"Late start," she said, wishing he'd go on holding her; in fact, wishing they could sneak off to his bedroom or hers and make love again. Spending all night and most of a day in bed with David had used her body better than it had ever been used before. And it had shut off her mind. Without worries, without burdens, she had been able to experience her body and his, to relax into pleasure in a way she never had before. Nina knew that release had been possible because she trusted David.

The trust, too, was easier, deeper than anything she'd felt in the past. A reluctant sigh accompanied her slipping out of his arms and returning to the kitchen stool.

He smiled. "I like hearing that. Makes a man feel wanted."

"Oh, you are." She picked up her spoon, swirled it through the oatmeal. "But this is a workday, and I assume you've come home to discuss a very important function you want me to arrange. We can go Indian this time if you like. There's a lovely woman from Mumbai in Bubby's building. She's ninety now, but very spry. I'll see if she's available to help cater."

A high-beam smile lit the handsome face that looked as if it had never had a hard knock. "Funny. You're very sassy, Miss Baxter."

She batted her lashes at him. "My boss likes it."

Taking the stool beside hers, he grinned down. "Yes, he does."

They could have grown awkward with each when her kids had come home Saturday night, but the transition back to family life had been far, far easier than Nina would have believed. David had not flirted or tried to see Nina in private; he hadn't expected her to sneak into his bed with her kids in the house. His behavior in front of her children hadn't changed at all. She was grateful.

But he had left her a note tucked into a corner of her bathroom mirror Sunday night. It had read simply, *Miss you, Beautiful.*

This was the first time she'd seen David since she'd found the paper, so she said now, "Thank you for my note."

He cast her an admirably blank look. "I'm sorry, Miss Baxter, we're all about business here. Unless you're referring to a memo, I'm afraid I can't discuss my personal life with an employee."

Nina smiled, just a tad smugly. He was being flip,

but the truth was he couldn't afford to ignore the impact their being lovers might have on his business life any more than she could ignore the effect on her children. Fortunately Nina had already decided on an eminently sensible plan. In fact, it was more than sensible; it was exciting.

She, Bubby and Janet had worked so well together in the kitchen that at one point Nina had mentioned they should all go into the catering business. Janet's eyes had lit with interest until she'd realized Nina had spoken tongue-in-cheek. But during the past twenty-four hours, Nina had decided the idea of starting her own business was nothing to laugh at. Why not party planning? Fun affairs with a sense of humor or a sense of elegance, but always at a respectable price.

Three Yentas. That's what they could call their firm. And in addition to party planning, they would provide hot, wonderful meals for busy people to purchase on a daily basis. David would continue to be her client, but he'd contract her as he would any other independent businessperson. He would no longer be her boss. Judging from the response they'd received after his party, they'd be busier than they needed to be in no time.

And, Nina would be able to move out.

Since being widowed, Janet lived alone in a house that she claimed was far too quiet. Nina hadn't asked her yet, but she had a feeling the other woman would agree to a work-rent situation.

Nina had always known she wanted something more than office work. Now she could pursue a career, a business of her own that truly excited her, *and* she could pursue a relationship with David without raising eyebrows. They could go out on dates, for crying out loud!

"What, I wonder, is making you smile?" David's voice rolled softly into her thoughts.

"I was thinking about how much everyone enjoyed Friday night."

He leaned toward her, close to her neck, where she felt his lips graze her ear. "*I* certainly did."

The first whispering touch made her breathless. One minute she was excited to tell him about her plans for the future; the next, she was excited about him.

"I'm sorry," she said, controlling her voice as much as possible, "but, as you pointed out, I'm not at liberty to discuss private affairs in a business setting. You'll have to— Oh!"

David swept an arm under her legs and lifted her into his arms. Nina grinned as he carried her from the kitchen. Her arms curled around his neck. "This is highly unacceptable behavior from a boss."

"You got that right," he growled.

"I don't suppose we're heading to the office for a little dictation?"

"Did I ask you to bring a pen?"

"I didn't finish my oatmeal."

He stopped and frowned down at her. She hid her

smile as he wrestled with good manners and a man's desire. When he looked at her closely enough to notice the faint curl of her lips, he carried her to the refrigerator, yanked open the door, told her to grab a can of whipped cream and a jar of peanut butter, then kicked the door closed.

"Peanut butter?" Nina hooked a brow as she balanced the jar and the can of whipped cream on her stomach.

Jaw set with determination, David didn't look down as he strode to his bedroom. "Trust me."

"Oh yes, that is soooo…mmmmm. Why is it so good like this?" Nina asked from her place in the middle of David's bed.

"It's the freedom. And the honesty." He reached into the jar of peanut butter with a forefinger, as Nina had been doing for the past few minutes, pulled up a neat blob and ate it slowly. "My guess is you've been using bread because you thought you had to. Now, for the first time, you realize there are no rules."

"God, you're smart." She licked her finger clean. "No rules for peanut butter." Running her tongue thoroughly over her lips, she shook her head. "You've shown me a whole new world, Mr. Hanson."

Grinning and sticky, they leaned forward to kiss. The sheet and thin blanket on David's bed were puddled around Nina's waist. The peanut butter was a concession to the fact that he'd interrupted her breakfast, but the whipped cream…

Ahhhh, the things David Hanson could do with a can of whipped cream…. It was enough to make a pastry chef blush.

David was also naked beneath the covers, which dipped low enough for Nina to see the silky hair that trailed from his flat belly to the V of his legs.

"Is this why you came home from work?" she asked, shamelessly batting her lashes.

"I came home to talk," David said, replacing the lid on the peanut-butter jar and leaning over to set it on the end table. He glanced wryly at the bare breasts that had occupied him for the past hour. "I got distracted."

Lightly tackling her, he pressed her down to the bed. Brushing blond curls from her eyes, he spoke softly.

"I'm probably going to bungle this, so hear me out before you say anything, okay?"

Bemused by the frown that drew one thin line between his brows, she nodded.

David reached for one of her hands, raised it to his lips. "Making love with you has been a revelation. You're loving, generous, shy one minute and wild the next." He narrowed his eyes. "Which is a very big turn-on, by the way." He slid his fingers through hers till their palms touched. "I love what just happened, but…" His pause tapped a fissure of worry into

Nina's mind. "I came home to tell you I don't want to sneak around like a couple of kids. I'm too old for that. Conducting a relationship in secret..." He shook his head. "It isn't going to work for me, Nina."

Nina's stomach lurched. Was he about to give her the brush-off? She tried to pull her hand back, but he held fast. "Let me make it clear up front that I do not plan to give up sex with you. But living together, working together, sleeping together—it's thorny."

Suddenly she understood: He really was going to fire her.

Nina wasn't a hundred-percent certain whether she should hit him or kiss him. She didn't like the idea of being fired for sleeping with the boss, but giving up the job—not him—was exactly her plan, too.

"I've been thinking—"

"I've given it some thought—"

They spoke at the same time.

"You first," Nina said.

Releasing her hand, David let his fingers play in the dip between her collarbones. "I have a new job for you. It's big."

He'd found her a different job? "What is it?"

"I want you to plan another party. But this one has nothing to do with Hanson's."

Nina's concern turned to anticipation. "Oh!" She smiled. "Hey, Mr. Hanson, I think we may be on the same wavelength."

He took a breath, held it a moment. "I hope so."

With his index finger, David traced a path between her breasts. "This party will be the biggest I've ever thrown. I know you worry about budgets—"

"On principle—"

"But this time there's no holding back. I mean it. I want this to be a front-page affair."

Nina was starting to get excited, and not only because David's fingers sent shivers racing over her skin. His party could dovetail perfectly with her idea. It could be Three Yentas' first official job.

"How many guests?"

"I'm not sure about the details yet. We'll have to hammer that out as we go along. But I'd like it to take place outdoors…if the guest of honor agrees."

"Who's your guest of honor?"

David rolled over Nina in a most unbusinesslike way. He stared down, looking as serious as she'd ever seen him.

"You."

The moment had not gone at all the way he'd planned.

David had never before asked anyone to marry him. He'd never come close. If he had, perhaps he'd have planned the moment more effectively: champagne, roses, an evening out. His proposal certainly couldn't have gone any worse.

When he'd finally blurted the words, "Let's get

married," Nina had looked like he'd asked her to bungee jump…without the cord.

Now the two of them stood across the room from each other, buttoning their clothes. She'd jumped out of bed first to get dressed, and he'd followed—not a good omen. Seemed that a successful marriage proposal ought to lead to *un*dressing.

Tucking his shirttail into his trousers, he waited for her to snap her jeans before he said, "I take it the answer is no?"

She winced at his tone. "This is happening a little fast, don't you think? I mean we just started…"

"Sleeping together?" he supplied when she stumbled. He heard the sarcasm in his voice, couldn't keep it out.

"Yes." Nina's expression held a mix of pain and frustration. "We haven't even had a first date, David. The word *premature* does come to mind." She shoved a hand into her hair. "I mean, what did you think? That out of the clear blue you'd announce you want to be a father and husband, and I'd jump up and say, 'Yippee, where's the ring?'"

Yes, he'd thought that. That was exactly how he'd pictured it.

He knew it was time to back down, let her have some space. In business, he'd always known when to ease off the pedal and when to go full throttle. He couldn't find that same willingness here. He felt only the drive to turn a no into a yes. At least to a maybe.

It was as if her refusal were turning his blood into something toxic, something caustic that burned with every beat of his heart.

"Let's say we back up." He tried to measure his tone, to sound more equable than he felt. "Let's say we begin again, start going on actual dates. We'll slow everything way down. Can you see yourself getting married this year? Next year?"

It was the wrong question. She didn't like it, and it made him sound pathetic as hell, but he couldn't seem to take it back. Before she started speaking, he knew he wouldn't want to hear the answer.

Like a cornered cat, ready to jump or hiss, Nina said, "I've been married once already. I don't know if I ever want to marry again. If I did, it wouldn't be for a very long time. Maybe after Zach and Izzy are in college." Her eyes entreated him to understand. "My family's welfare has to come first."

She raised her chin in a gesture that bespoke resolution, and though her expression was not without compassion, David knew it was over, just like that. He felt a knife slice his heart as easily as if it were slipping through butter. He'd made a critical mistake; he was not part of her family, yet for an unguarded moment he had allowed himself to believe he could be.

He loved Nina. He was sure of it. He'd seen a new life with her in his arms, and it had felt so good and so right he hadn't wanted to spend another minute alone.

When he'd rushed home, he'd been thinking about his needs, not hers. She didn't need him to make her feel loved or cherished or *full*. She had that already. In one form or another she'd always had it.

He was the one who'd driven through his life with his gauge on empty and hadn't even realized it until now.

Sensations he couldn't identify, wasn't sure he wanted to identify, poured into his chest like blood.

The last time he'd felt this desperate, this hungry, his parents had been packing for yet another business trip that would keep them away for yet another Thanksgiving. David had been six; George had been a young man and had accompanied their folks. While their father and George had taken the luggage to the car, David had flung himself against his mother's legs and begged her to stay with him. He was going to be a Native American in the Thanksgiving play at school.

His mother had been gentle, but firm. She'd reminded him that they all had jobs to do: his was to be an Indian in the play; hers was to travel with Daddy. The housekeeper and the nanny had had to peel David away. The day of the play, he'd thrown up on a pilgrim and had had to lie on a cot backstage until the show was all over.

He hadn't thought of that in years. It was a helluva memory to have now. Classic maudlin, old-wound crap. The kind of thing Oprah would eat up and a hundred-and-fifty-dollar-an-hour shrink would yawn over.

But enough to remind him that he would never, ever be that desperate again. He'd been too hungry with Nina, moved too fast.

And he'd forgotten that you couldn't take what someone else didn't have to give.

Chapter Fifteen

"I got some news for you." Bubby hovered over Nina, a dish towel in one of the knotty-boned hands she'd plunked on her hips.

"What's the news?" Seated on Bubby's over-stuffed chair, which hadn't been reupholstered since 1979, Nina let her legs dangle over the arm and divided her attention between the bag of white-cheddar popcorn on her lap, the *Fear Factor* Miss USA episode she was watching on her grandmother's thirty-two-inch TV, and Bubby.

On the large screen, a bikini-clad beauty was about to be covered in a garden-fresh medley of maggots, hissing cockroaches and a few nonpoisonous (cross our fingers and hope to die) scorpions. Given her mood, Nina thought it was a sissy challenge.

Bubby picked the remote control off the edge of the seat cushion, near Nina's butt, and muted the terrified screams of Miss District of Columbia.

"The news is this," she said, glaring daggers at her granddaughter. "There ain't enough room in this apartment for the kids, me, you and your pity party. You want to sit around looking bored and depressed, go sit in the apartment lobby. It's all Prozac and checkers down there—you'll fit right in."

"I'm not bored and I'm not depressed," Nina argued, though she'd been both for nearly a week. "I'm just tired from job hunting, and you're making me miss *Fear Factor*."

She had trouble meeting Bubby's gaze.

My family's welfare has to come first. The words she'd thrown at David almost seven days ago returned to clang through her head once every half hour, as reliable as clockwork. She was getting quite a headache.

She'd felt so smug, so righteous when she'd uttered the nobler-than-God statement. No one could argue with such a priority.

She hadn't heard from David since that day, and she realized now she wasn't going to. Probably not ever. And that wasn't what she'd intended. She hadn't meant to end their relationship completely; only to manage it a little because he was getting way ahead of himself and didn't even realize it. She'd been right not to leap into a decision about the rest of their lives.

Maybe that worked on TV reality shows…no, not even there.

She shoveled a handful of popcorn into her mouth. She'd been the voice of reason that day, and she wasn't going to let Bubby or anyone else make her doubt herself.

So why did she feel so lousy?

When she'd crunched the kernels enough to allow herself to speak, she said, "I'm sorry we're taking up so much room here, Bubby. I know this place isn't big enough for three extra people. As soon as Janet Daitch gets back from visiting her family in Des Moines, I'll ask if we can move in with her."

"*Psshhh!*" Bubby waved Nina's comment away. "Since when is room for family a problem? Room, I got plenty of. What I don't got is a granddaughter with an ounce of good sense when it comes to men!"

Nina swung her legs off the arm of the chair so quickly, popcorn spilled onto her lap. "What?"

"You heard." Bubby glanced to the bedroom where Izzy and Zach were spread out, doing their homework. Crossing to the sofa, she sat and pointed to her own temple. "My memory is the only part of me that never ages. Details stand out in my mind, and when I put them together I have a clear picture."

Nina longed for an excuse to get up, to sidestep the sharp blue gaze and whatever point Bubby was about to make, but she knew her grandmother's it's-got-to-be-said look; leaving now would only postpone the inevitable. Working a piece of popcorn from between her front teeth, Nina hunched her shoulders and hoped Bubby would be quick.

"I remember one detail in particular from the summer you turned thirteen," the seventy-seven-year-old began, traveling farther back in time than Nina had anticipated. "There was a boy who moved in next door to your parents' house. Two years older than you and thinking more about his first car than his first girl, I think. But you—" Bubby rolled her head. "Such devotion! You wrote his name on napkins, your father's newspaper, even on a pancake once in boysenberry syrup. Always with little hearts and sometimes a poem. Except on the pancake. You remember?"

Nina was stunned. She hadn't thought about that in years. "I remember I had a crush on a boy named Ben."

Bubby nodded, smoothing her housecoat over her knees. "You were going to ask him to the fall dance when school started. Then your parents flew back east...."

Bubby didn't have to finish that thought. Nina would never forget the phone call to the airline, the official who had come to the door, the feeling of wanting to scream and never stop.

"You cried for two days," Bubby remembered, "then, 'Bubby, don't worry,' you told me, 'I'll take care of you.'" For the first time in a long, long time, Bubby's eyes looked older, worn. "It was supposed to be the other way around," she said. "After that, no more school dance. No more hearts over anyone's name."

Nina stirred uncomfortably, wishing she could keep memories of that time stored in a dark corner of her mind. "I suppose even a thirteen-year-old can have a sense of priorities."

"I suppose." Bubby smoothed her housecoat over her knees. "I got one more story."

Nina was absolutely certain she didn't have the strength to hear it. She pointed to the muted TV. "Miss South Carolina just swallowed a maggot. I'm going to turn the sound up."

Bubby managed to beat her to the remote. "One more, then you can watch Miss Silicone Injections eat *treyf*." She sat back down. "You were too young to remember your grandfather, my Max, may his memory be a blessing. I was eighteen when I met him, and within a week I knew I wanted to get married. A real love affair, and we wanted kids right away, even though we were so young we could barely afford to pay rent on one room. 'There's always a way,' Max said. And so I got pregnant, and a happier girl you never saw. But the baby, a daughter, came too early, and the doctors couldn't save her. Back then was different. Today—" she shrugged "—who knows?"

This was one story Nina had never heard, and as she watched her grandmother, she saw the moistness in her aged eyes. Here was a story Bubby had found too painful to retell.

"I had prayed and prayed for my daughter to be saved. I named her Liba, 'my heart.' When she died, my heart went with her. No one could talk to me, not even Max. 'We'll try again,' he said, but I didn't want to." She shook her head, closing her eyes briefly. "Such a thing, so unthinkable, had happened once. God forbid it should happen again." She shook her head. "'It would kill me,' I told Max, and I said if he wanted to marry someone else, someone who still wanted children, I would understand."

"He loved you too much to let you go," Nina said, wanting to smooth the pain from Bubby's face.

Bubby opened her eyes. They held all the sadness and all the sweetness of seven decades when she said, "He loved life too much to let me stop living. He would have stuck with me no matter what, but then he said, 'If we give up, Rayzel, we won't know what comes next.' He always looked forward, and I loved him too much to ask him to stop looking."

She reached out, ran a finger softly along Nina's cheek. "What came next was your father. And so much joy." Watching Nina closely, she clucked her tongue softly. "I know what you're thinking, and it's true. I've buried a daughter, and I've buried a son, so where's the happy ending to this story, hmm?" She touched her finger to Nina's nose. "You. And Zach and Izzy. Now you're what comes next, and I'm so grateful I didn't miss you.

"What can we do but love anyway, Nina? We accept how painful life can be and love anyway. It's the most faithful thing a person can do."

"I love my kids," Nina said in a hoarse whisper.

"I know that." Bubby reached for her necklace, gold with a quarter-sized medallion. Working the clasp free, she let the gold puddle in her hand, then held it out to her granddaughter. "My father bought me this on a trip to Israel."

Nina knew what it was without looking: a Torah scroll with the engraved words Be Guarded and Protected.

Gently but with firm intention, Bubby closed Nina's fingers around the gift. "To remind you that you're always safe. And that no risk is too big when it's made for love."

Bubby leaned back, obviously tired. "Draw pretty hearts around some special boy's name again, my Ninele. And draw a few of the hearts a little broken, a little worse for the wear." She nodded her grayed head. "It's okay. They'll be as pretty as the others."

Rising with a soft groan, she headed toward the kitchen. "I'm going to get hot cocoa and raspberry *rugelach* for the kids. So the studying will be sweet."

Nina sat on the chair, the Torah pendant in her closed fist. As she felt the rim of the gold circle press into her palm, she realized Bubby hadn't offered her answers, really. Only courage to live with the questions.

Eleven days after Nina and the kids had moved out, David felt sure he wanted to sell the condo.

Izzy had left a pair of pink sunglasses in the TV room. A corner of Zach's *The Ocean World of Jacques Cousteau* poked out from beneath the desk in the library.

David figured he'd find things for the next few weeks. He considered selling the place lock, stock and barrel. Let someone else find pieces of Nina's family.

Maybe he would start over somewhere outside of Chicago. He began to wonder why he stayed here anyway, why he made himself crazy trying to save Hanson Media Group. None of George's kids were interested in the business. Even Jack would love to get out. So why hold on? For whom?

In the days since Nina's unqualified rejection of his proposal, he'd decided she was right: He'd jumped the gun in telling her he wanted to get married right away and had probably come across like a stalker in the process.

He'd put them all in an impossible situation, the kind from which there was no going back. Now Nina and the kids were gone, and he was left to pick up the pieces of a life he no longer liked.

When the doorbell rang at seven-fifteen on Friday evening, he'd been about to carry his heated Healthy Choice Tenderloin Strips in Gravy to the kitchen counter, where he would doubtlessly stare at it a few minutes then throw it down the garbage disposal. That had been his dinner routine for the past week. He had no appetite to eat alone and no desire to ask anyone to join him.

It was not a hardship, therefore, to leave the TV dinner on the kitchen counter and plod to the door. Maybe Jack had decided to drop in. Uncharacteristically, his nephew had shown up twice in the past week to discuss the reading of his father's will and how to ensure the presence of his two younger brothers.

As David reached for the knob, he decided that if it was Jack, he'd make his nephew go out for pizza and beers. The thought of throwing his frozen dinner out *before* he wasted time staring at it perked him up a bit.

When he opened the door, however, no one was on his threshold or in the hall. Mystified, and disappointed, David was about to succumb to solitude when he noticed a large ivory envelope lying at his feet. The words *Private Invitation* were printed across the front in red felt-tip marker.

Bringing the envelope inside, he stared at it until it felt heavy on his palm. Withdrawing a hand-printed card, he read, *Please join us on the rooftop at 7:30 p.m. Dress casual.* The invitation was unsigned. If this was some impromptu get-to-know-the-neighbors party, he really wanted to pass. Even gelatinous brown gravy would be better than small talk.

When he reread the card, however, David noticed that the lettering was very round and very careful—a child's printing.

His heart pounded, leaving a pain with every beat. *Could be some other kids,* he told himself, *maybe kids in the building. Could even be a practical joke.* But he glanced at his watch and headed for his bedroom, where he changed his shirt, brushed his hair and teeth, and told himself not to be an idiot. Even if Zach and Izzy were on his roof—and why would they be?—Nina could be miles away.

He took the elevator, then a short flight of stairs,

making himself walk in measured, deliberate paces. When he reached the door that lead to the rooftop, he stopped and read a sign, again hand-lettered, and that's when his body tripped into high gear.

Family Shabbat. Please Enter.

He reached for the door, jerked it open and crossed the threshold onto a rooftop that had been decorated with flowers, a folding table covered by a blue cotton cloth with painted handprints, and a string of twinkle lights that glowed softly against an evening sky streaky with orange and lavender.

Zach ran and Izzy skipped over to him.

"Did you get your invitation?"

"We dropped it off!"

"We had to run to the elevator so you wouldn't see us!"

"We wanted you to be surprised."

Excited, they tumbled over each other's sentences. They didn't hug him, though, and it shocked David to realize how much he wanted them to. He'd become so accustomed in his life to handshakes—starting with his own father—that when Zach and Izzy had first started hugging him hello, he hadn't known quite how to respond. Then he'd realized the only response necessary was to fill his arms with them, and he'd looked forward to coming home in the evenings.

Tonight, they maintained a tentative distance, despite their excitement. There had already been too much time and space between them all; the affection wasn't easy now. He knew he could open his arms first, that they might close the distance if he did. But he was scared to do it; scared they might not respond and even more scared that he would hold on too tight if they did. The realization shamed him.

He glanced up, over their heads. Bubby stood at the cloth-covered table. Only Bubby. A cauldron of disappointment bubbled hotly in his stomach. Nina wasn't here. This wasn't reconciliation. She hadn't decided they should begin again as friends…perhaps go on a couple of dates, see if they could make something fit.

Idiot, he castigated himself even as he dredged up a smile for Bubby. He looked again at the kids, realizing that staying here would be painful for him, but that he owed it to them to try. When Izzy tentatively took his hand to lead him to the table, he concentrated on how good the simple gesture felt, rather than on how much he would miss it in the days to come.

Bubby smiled as he approached. Several short candles in mismatched holders huddled together atop the decorative tablecloth. He was going to have a difficult time not picturing Nina, how she had glowed in the candlelight the evening he'd first witnessed this simple, haunting ceremony. He was about to ask Bubby if the rooftop Shabbat had been her idea, when he heard a sound behind him.

Her hair, as blond as yarn an angel had spun and covered by the same lace she'd worn last time, was the first thing David noticed. And then her smile.

Small, aching in its hopefulness, Nina's pink lips curved to match the question in her eyes.

"Thank you for coming," she murmured. *Will you*

stay? She didn't voice that part, but he understood and nodded around the catch in his throat.

There was no more talking then. Nina started by striking a match and lighting a candle, like last time. And like last time, David felt the edges of his body blur until he was part of the light and song, part of Bubby and Izzy and Zach. He tried to let his mind and body soften until he became part of Nina, too, but that was more difficult, more effortful. When she waved her hands over the candles, drawing the light to her, and sang the prayers and touched her children's heads to bless them, she was the hub of the family wheel, and David knew she belonged to the others.

He wondered why she'd brought him here. If this was an apology for ending abruptly, a way to say, "We can still be friends," he wasn't sure he could muster gratitude. Hanging onto the edge of their family circle was too painful.

The time to light the remainder of the candles—one for each of them—came, and Nina told her family what tonight's theme was. "Courage. When you light your candle tonight, tell one thing you were afraid to do this past week, and one thing you're going to try in the week ahead."

Bubby went first and said, "I'm going to tell Flo Melcher she needs new dentures. A friend don't let another friend wear teeth from 1962."

Zach talked about standing up for a kid who was being ostracized at school, and Izzy said she wasn't going to let Beth Knox cheat off her spelling test anymore even if Beth did tell Danny Hafner that

Izzy thought he was cute. Nina's eyes widened over that one, and David figured there was going to be a talk between mother and daughter later tonight.

There were two candles left—his and Nina's. By tacit agreement, Bubby and the children headed for the rooftop door.

Surprised, David watched them go then looked back to Nina, whose chest rose and fell on a nervous breath. "My turn," she said, holding the candle in front of herself. "I'm not sure I'll be able to top Bubby and the Flo Melcher commitment, but here goes...."

Her gaze held his as she explained, "Last week I was afraid to tell you the truth when you asked me to marry you. I panicked and said the first thing that came to mind—that it was too soon to talk about marriage. But that isn't why I said no."

Even as blood rushed through David's veins, his heart felt as if it skidded to a stop. Did he want to hear this?

"I should have told you that I care about you. That I like being with you. That I like it so much, I could hardly breathe this past week when I thought I might never see you again."

David would have taken her in his arms at that moment, he would have let the single admission be enough, but courage was not a job to be left half-done, and Nina had more to say.

"I dreamed of you, you know. For years I imagined someone strong and steady, someone whose love would make the world feel small and safe." She smiled with awareness. "It wasn't a good dream. It wasn't life. Life's the thing I'm most afraid of.

"I thought I was being smart, loving just a few people—Bubby and Izzy and Zach. Damage control, you know? Fewer people, less pain. But now you're here."

In the glow of the candlelight, she wore all her feelings—uncertainty, fear, hope—in her eyes. "I don't want to love and have it not work out between us, David. But I'm even more afraid of losing you without a fight."

"You're not going to lose me." David did reach for her then, pulling her close, holding her with a fierce protectiveness. He'd never felt such blessed relief. "I promise you that."

Nina put her arms around him, reached up to caress his neck. "You can't promise that. But that's okay." She pushed back to meet his gaze. "I can't promise you, either. But I can promise to remember how I feel in this moment and to remember always why I love you."

Taking a step away, she tilted her candle to one of the dancing flames. The unlit wick crackled to life. "I promise that whenever letting go seems easier, I'll dig for the courage to hang on."

Placing her candle next to the others, she sealed the vow.

"Letting go is never going to be an issue, not for us," David claimed with all the brash male assurance her love brought to life.

Nina laid her palm, cool and smooth and calming,

against his cheek, and he felt his heart sink a little, felt his assuredness waver.

"I don't know much about courage, Nina. If I did, I'd have waited to ask you to marry me. I'd have taken you out to dinner and danced until three. We'd have sat by the river and talked about all the years we shared the same office but not the same life."

He shook his head, traced a long curl with the tip of his finger and whispered, "I rushed because you're everything I want. I was afraid to give you time to think, because I didn't want you to realize that I need you a hell of a lot more than you need me."

If he thought the truth might disappoint or scare her, he was wrong. "Ask me again, David," she said in a whisper that was all she seemed able to manage. "Ask me again to get married and be your family."

Looking at her with all the solemnity and all the purpose of a man who had found his calling in life, he said, "Marry me. Marry me now or marry me later. I'm not afraid to wait, because you know what I've realized? Becoming a family is a serious business. And I'm going to devote the rest of my life to it."

This time she initiated the kiss. Its promise was strong and sure.

"I think I'd like another baby," she murmured when they broke apart, grinning as David's brows shot up. "Your baby." He was speechless. "What are you thinking?"

"I think we should have two."

Arching back, Nina laughed, a joyful, worry-free sound.

David's gaze fell on the single wick that remained unlit. Leaning to his left, he raised the candle, tipping it toward one whose flame already burned bright.

Eyes shining, Nina placed her hand atop his, and they lit the last candle together.

* * * * *

Look for the next chapter in the
Special Edition continuity,
THE FAMILY BUSINESS,
THE BABY DEAL
by
Victoria Pade
Playboy Andrew Hanson has spent years
running from responsibility. But when a
night of passion results in unplanned
pregnancy, Andrew must convince beautiful
Delia McCray that he is worthy of marriage
and fatherhood—despite being a younger man!
Available March 2006,
wherever Silhouette Books are sold.

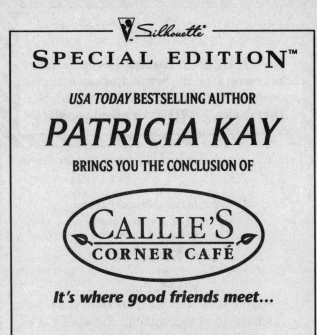